GW00686400

More
Gallimaufry

A second collection of poems,
short stories and memoirs

Totnes Library Writers Group

Bookword

Published in 2021 by Bookword
www.bookword.co.uk

Copyright © Totnes Library Writers Group

The right of Totnes Library Writers Group to be identified as the authors of this work has been asserted in accordance with the Copyright, Design and Patents Act 1988

ISBN 978-1-9996286-1-1

Printed and bound by Nick Walker printing Ltd, Kingsbridge

Cover image: Devon Landscape by Fiona Green
Cover design and typesetting: Caroline Guillet
Colour illustrations: Julie Mullen
Line drawings: Barbara Childs

More
Gallimaufry

Contents

Marie Chesham

Thelma Portch

Contributors   152

Introduction

The Totnes Library Writers Group could be described as an interesting and eclectic group of talented writers who meet once a fortnight in a small market town in South Devon.

It was formed in September 2013 by the then Head Librarian, Chris Alton, at Totnes Library and met for the first time in the old School Hall in the Mansion. A large, and very mixed group of published and beginner writers, it quickly became apparent that this was to be no ordinary 'writing group'. No leader emerged. The group wanted to share work but didn't want to write together all the time. No theme for work was given each session, no compulsory payments or subscriptions, no pressure. Ideas were floated, accepted or rejected and a strong ethos developed that still sustains the group today. Writers, whatever their ability or experience, are welcomed and their work met with respect and enthusiasm. The group has developed only one rule: no writer is allowed to deprecate themselves or their writing and attempts to break this rule (however cleverly worded) are met with group remonstration.

The Totnes Library Writers Group meets to share and discuss. But while structure may be lacking – it only has an excellent Treasurer and a super efficient Keeper of the Email – decisions are still reached organically and the group continues to exist through its will and its members' care and support of each other.

Within this group there are a number of published writers, a Bard and a former Great Bard. Between them, they have created a series of workshops led by talented writers from around the country; published their first anthology, *Gallimaufry*, in 2015, which was brought about by the hard work and dedication of Fiona Murray; and organised a successful writing festival, to encourage and support local writers. Giving opportunities to experience all aspects of writing, the *Write Now Totnes!* festival ended with a poetry slam that introduced many new poets to this exciting form of extreme poeting. They have also survived the pandemic with the same drive and determination to inspire and promote a love of writing and to support and care for each other.

If you're moving to South Devon you may feel that you want to join them. You would be welcome...

Sanctuary

Jackie Juno

I am Priestess of the Powder Puff experiment
Alice in the graveyard
tripping through doorways
into test-tube universes.

Cast away
iron-robed
tasting blood
meandering
moonwandering alone,
a Chapel of Chaos.

Eventually

I find sanctuary

in my sugar cane pump house heart.

Four wolves Spell Joy

Jackie Juno

Swallows are sewing sky –
one just dive-bombed into this poem
and I have surround sound tweets.
Blue tits punctuate the air between birch and beech,
gliding pigeons are on a mission
and on the wagtailed lawn
there is a unison of foliage.

What does the urgent breeze bring?
A reminder of our powerlessness,
anger at our crassness,
our scarring.

I'm halfway down the Sticklepathfaultline
and even after this century's warnings
we have learnt little.

I have an ear for children.
They have not been bound by our history,
they know we have failed
in our care for the serpent, the canary, the dove.

Watch the weather.
Gather each perfect cloud to anoint your marble throat.
Pluck apple blossom to adorn your precious hair.
Make every dewdrop a jewel.
One magpie spells sorrow
but four wolves spell joy.
Yes, cry; yes, keen – but also
open wide your mouth
and sing.

Obsidians in Moon

Jackie Juno

I keep owls in my head.
And at night when they wake
I borrow their eyes, just for a few seconds
before they wrestle, agitated,
in my skull.
Then I have to let them out or it gets really messy.
Silently they fly out, ghosts in the dark,
to prey on tiny quivering thoughts
I've let loose during daylight.

It's been raining stars again.
The owls like that.
They love new stuff; it's all an adventure to them.
Sickled claws grasp at branches, make runic
the trees I created
from hopes and dreams.
The owls skuwee to each other.
This spooks the woman who works in the opticians.
Scurrying down the lane,
she's been moonlighting again.
Hisses escape from those sharp beaks,
beaks desperate to tear flesh.

I don't want to go to bed. I follow them out
into the monochrome meadow
where nothing makes sense,
where blood is the common language
and mud is my ally.
Scraggy feathers are waterlogged,
we walk on a crescent blade.
He mustn't know I'm out, he'd worry.

But I can't go back now. I'm on a mission.
When owls call, you listen.
I just want you all to know,
if I don't make it –
I chose this.

Recipe for Healing

Jackie Juno

I found this recipe in my great-great-great grandmother's diary. It had been lost for over a hundred years, which is a shame, because the mothers between me and her could've done with it.

Take the sharp knife from between your shoulder blades.

Wipe clean with that magic cloth your best friend gifted you.

Halve the lemons that were thrown at you. Squeeze them and retain the juice for later.

Gather all those bitter missiles of olives and dried fruits.

Soak them for 7 years in Dartmoor spring water.

Blend in local honey at Beltane.

Every August, add rose petals from your own garden.

Stir clockwise at each winter solstice.

Drain and discard the water from the steeped missiles. You now have a bowl of plump soft fruits. Add these to the lemon juice.

Place two dessert spoonfuls of the fruit into a tall glass of ice. Add your favourite botanical gin.

Share with the good people in your life.

Celebrate.

Give thanks you haven't turned out like her.

Hot

Jackie Juno

Best summer ever, they said. The earth cracked. The grass withered where it stood, turned brown. The soil was terracotta dry.

We played with the hosepipe in the garden, five girlie squeals heralded the sweet shock of cold. Until they banned hosepipes.

Dad's white Capri got filthier with those August weeks. My hair got thick and matted, slabs of frizz on my head, skin brown as a nut. We found new ways to save water.

Then Jo and I went to live above the shop with Mom. Suddenly there was no garden, no friends, no school. Mom busy in the shop all day, we would argue upstairs in the baking air. Nothing to do, nowhere to go. Lolled about on the sofa in the blinding heat.

I missed the other sisters, missed the sounds of the hairdryer drowning out Ziggy, missed hearing Jen's Mini coughing to life every morning, missed the smell of Steph's curries seeping into every crevice of clothing, missed Tracey's Supremes soundtrack as she got ready to go out.

Yes, and I missed Dad.

But I had the electric pink solace of the soft fake fur cushion on my bed which Steph had given me for my birthday, and the hand-me-downs that I had now made mine: faded denim skirt and waistcoat, thigh-high striped socks, platform clogs and cheesecloth blouse.

The summer of '76. So hot the earth cracked. So hot you couldn't move. So dry you couldn't breathe. We were stifled.

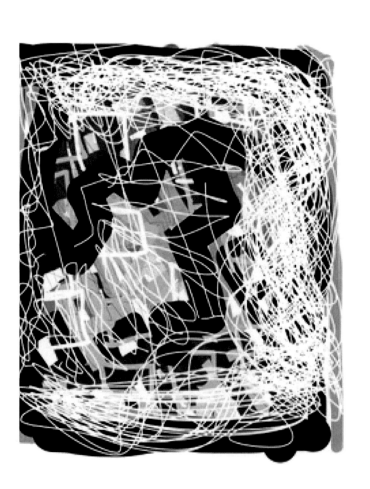

Twenty Guineas

David Barker

Nobody had told the rain to stop, just because the fighting was over. It seemed that summer would never arrive in this part of Belgium, and for many on this battlefield, there would never be another. A man with brown hair, brown eyes, and brown clothes was trying to pull a glistening leather boot off somebody who would never use it again. The mud beneath the corpse was deep and hungry. Another tug and the man fell backwards as the boot finally surrendered.

Something soft broke his fall. And groaned.

The man scrambled to his feet and turned to peer through the gloom of this late evening.

"Please. Help." A pale face amidst the sludge. Belonging to a person in an officer's uniform.

"Reckon I will help meself."

"They've already taken my valuables." The officer winced as the other man tugged at his braided jacket.

"Still got yer teeth, ain't you?"

"I have plenty of money back in Brussels. I'll furnish you with twenty guineas if you'll guard me this night."

"Twenty?" He whistled. "'Ow do I know you'll keep your word?" The man stood up and waved a knife through the air, testing its balance. "Easy to promise things, lying there in the shit, sun going down. I've seen what 'appens after battles. You lot trit-trot back to yer ladies. Forget the rest of us, privateers, living off second-hand boots and teeth."

"I, sir, am an officer of the Royal Dragoons. My word is like the British Army. Unbreakable, sir, unbreakable."

The looter paused. "We sure gave them Frenchies a taste of what for, didn't we?"

The officer looked around at the bodies. Once-bright uniforms, washed brown by the blood and the dirt and the setting sun; it was hard to tell the armies of the dead apart. "Damned close thing, I should say."

The other man's eyelids squeezed together. "Alright lieutenant, I'll keep ya safe. Nuffink will happen to you while ol' Bert is by your side."

"I'm grateful to you." The officer stared at the little man. "Where's the rest of your troop?"

"We was holding the centre when Bony's Himperial Guard themselves pitched in. Right at the end." The man swallowed as if something distasteful were in his mouth. "Most of me mates were 'acked to pieces. I were lucky to get away."

"Damned good job the blue Prince turned up when he did." The officer reached out with his arm and scratched where his knee joined the carved wood.

"What's yer story then?"

"I'll remind you to address me as an officer, corporal."

The man ducked his head slightly. "Apologies, lieutenant."

"My story, eh? Yes, it might pass the time. Be a good man and fetch me some brandy first, will you? Deuced cold lying here. And see if you can find something to eat. Breakfast was an awfully long time ago."

The soldier snapped to his feet. "Right you are, sir. Be as quick as I can."

The lieutenant leant back and exhaled. The plan was working, the English accent impeccable. He went over his backstory one more time in his head. Old Bert might have been easy to ensnare, but he was no fool. Any inconsistencies now could ruin the whole thing.

Bruxelles, j'arrive.

An Explanation

Fiona Green

Reckless rain!
Carelessly incontinent
You slither down my neck.
Tears from my eyes
Mimic your shape and formation;
Holding my pain in public view.

Lost in old patterns of remembrance
I see the repetition in my son's anguish
And can only stand by helpless, till he learns
That after rain
Comes quiet contemplation
And new opportunities for love.

The Poet in My Circle

Fiona Green

She sits quietly
No longer writing
"I have acceptance,"
She says.

I want to stir
Her energy again,
Hungry for more joy
From her pen.

When I was young
I moved with poets
Consigning their words
To normal currency.

Now I am old
I yearn for those times
To learn to treasure
What I once took for granted.

All the Blind Flowers

Fiona Green

The blind flowers' words
Scream to the silent forest
Awake: It is Spring!

Time to come alive

The old shadows of Winter
Recall
A darker time of grief

With memories of a dying man.

Come, lovely, soothing death
Transform my longing
Into a sacred form

Upon which to cast my eye.

A gorgeous thing,
An envy to my friends:
Escort me now

To feast on whole forgetfulness.

I need to leave the past behind
Where it belongs:
To start anew with gentleness

And summon strength, to be myself again.

The Spider Seeking Refuge

Fiona Green

Having eaten all my dreams,
You hang there, large on my diaphanous curtain
Your legs as lacy
As the patterns to which you cling
You master weaver.

My cut glass covers and traps you
Unwitting interloper,
So that I can move you
From the warmth of my sitting room
To the wet and cold of a wintry Totnes garden.

And now the deed is done
I reproach myself:
Thinking of other outsiders at our shores
Who look to some, as unacceptable as you
Yet, who also need a warm place to hibernate.

Under the Spindle Tree

Anne Morris

Sitting in the garden I see you in my mind's eye as you work away quietly at your tasks.

You spin stories from wisps of yarn, make us believe they are real, or would be, if we could only see them as you do.

You weave dreams, perhaps you find it hard to live in this world, needing sometimes to be in that other place.

You are often absent; where you go to is better, you say. It's a long-lost friend that you need to keep close.

You might no longer travel, time has put paid to that, but you're there always, in your mind; still present in those distant lands.

It's there you say your heart is, with people who still live close to the earth: close to how we all lived before civilisation stripped us of our ancient souls.

So you find your own way back – day after day.

You speak silently as you work, telling your stories as you place each thread.

The blossom is falling as I look up through the branches, and it will soon be a memory.

But you know how to keep memories alive. You sit each day lovingly threading magic into your tapestries.

They will remain, loved and cherished by those you leave behind; pictures of where you've been and what you've seen.

They're a reminder of who you are and who you've been. A traveller, who carries that love and those memories with her. A spinner and weaver of dreams.

Tiny Kisses

Carole Ellis

Tiny kisses following the curve of my inner thigh
Your hand warm on my neck, lifting my hair to trail kisses there.
Echoes of a time when we had a world of time – for lingering
caresses and playful adventures.

Now we look back remembering those past selves – fitter,
thinner, unfettered by the ticking clock and undaunted by
passing time.
Innocent, ignorant and full of hope.

Yet in that tortured, joyous moment when time explodes be-
tween us, I see in your eyes the scars that time has left
And love more deeply the you that loves me now
And cherish more keenly those tiny kisses following the curve of
my inner thigh.

Elderly Passions

Carole Ellis

When knees begin to creek
And elbows ache with rain,
When life seems done and over
It's easy to believe a mug of cocoa's just fine.

But now's the time to grasp life's nettle
And tear and gnaw and slurp.
For life is meant to be lived with passion
And you, my love, are mine.

What this is!

Carole Ellis

We met too late and fell too hard
For this to ever last.
Yet with each passing year we prove them wrong
Those who said you were a passing phase
And I your mid-life crisis.

I call you lover and you call me friend
We started in different places
But we wound up at this end
With battle scars and broken souls
And this thing that stands intact.

From every angle we glimpse a different face.
It can be cheap and sordid or glorious: standing the test of time
It lasts no matter what we do
It changes and it grows
This thing between us that we never meant to know.

There Are No Words

Carole Ellis

Like a single-handed round-the-world yachtsman returning to
harbour,
Like the Apollo 13 crew touching down in the ocean,
Like the safe arrival of a new born child,
Like cupped hands around a mug of hot tea on a cold night
when the last bus has been cancelled and the walk home has
been icy and treacherous.
I hold open my arms and enfold your trembling body,
feeling it pressed against the trembling of my own,
and there are no words.

There are no words.

Another Life

Carole Ellis

I dreamt I'd lived another life
Where we had never met
And woke with tears upon my pillow
And emptiness in my heart.

I dreamt I'd lived another life
Where we had met and married
And woke with tears upon my pillow
And longing in my heart.

For life can only be lived once
And too soon we make our choices
And so wake with pillows wet with tears
And sadness in our heart.

Marrows and Mayhem

Carole Ellis

Clutching the razor-sharp knife to her chest, Linda crept carefully forwards. The bright full moon that had lit her way now disappeared behind a cloud leaving thick darkness to slow her progress, but the path was so familiar that she had often said she could find her way in the dead of night. Putting out her hand, she felt cool skin just where skin was expected and that's when she began to stab, stab, stab....

The following morning chaos did not begin to express the horror and confusion that gripped the small village of Ample Bounding as news of the attack flew around it carried with the milk, the papers and the post. The police had arrived by the time Linda pushed her bicycle behind her shed and made herself comfortable on her old bench. Taking out her thermos flask and pouring her first cup of tea, she watched PC Brown scratching his head and looking shocked. Old Fred was trying to comfort a distraught Big Lou. Big Lou's sister, Tiny Tina – chairman of the judging committee – shook her head. "Frankly my lovely, that's only fit for – well, compost."

Big Lou howled in anguish, sinking to the ground and putting her arms around her beloved and now no longer potentially-prize-winning marrow that lay a tattered mess on the ground, its yellowish innards spilling about it for all to see.

"Why would anyone do this to me?" cried Big Lou, looking about her at the small crowd of on-lookers.

"Because you're a bloody cheat," muttered Linda as she put the cup back into her bag and, picking up her hoe, began to weed between her courgettes.

Later, when the last of the spectators had gone and the sad remains had been cleared away, Linda walked across to her friend.

"You've still some pretty mighty ones and the show's not for a couple of weeks," she said. "There's still a chance."

Big Lou sniffed, wiping her face on her sleeve. "There's no chance really. Even Mad Bob's got bigger marrows. Let's face it, Lindy, I'm done for."

Linda squeezed Lou's arm in a comforting manner. "There's always next year," she said and then walked back to her patch before her triumphant grin could give the game away.

The Annual Ample Bounding Show was the biggest event in the area. Villagers from far and wide entered flowers, vegetables and produce into this prestigious show and the prizes were not to be sniffed at. There was a hamper of groceries from Jenkins for the winner of the best flower arrangement and a side of pork from Lumstone's Butchers for the winner of the top prize of Biggest Marrow.

The only problem with the Ample Bounding Show was the Ample Bounding Judging Committee. Each one had their favourites, and traditions ruled. If you weren't in with the Judging Committee you simply didn't win.

Big Lou had won the prize for Biggest Marrow for the last fifteen years. Whilst Tiny Tina had only been judging for the last five years, their father, Malcolm had been head judge for twenty years before that. Every year Big Lou staggered away with the Lumstone's meat prize and just for once Linda wanted to be in with a chance.

She had planned a more surreptitious end for the marrow that Big Lou nurtured better than she did her husband: something more in keeping with the slow demise of Mr Wilkinson's prize-winning dahlias – what a shame that his secret tonic (if tested) would turn out to be more Weedol than comfrey. But last night Big Lou had left the allotment joking with Sid the Salad that she 'had it in the bag' this year and as Linda sat on her bench surrounded by her 'second rate' efforts, something black and angry came over her. She had taken up her pruning knife and ended Big Lou's chances for this year.

Linda didn't do flower arranging or preserve making – that was a bit girly for her – but she did love growing vegetables. This year her absolute best thing was her beetroots which was why a villager's Jack Russell had found its way on to a neighbouring plot. The dog had set to digging for all it was worth and in the process managed to destroy a vast quantity of prize-winning beetroots. No prize for Agnes this year! But a very good chance of one for Linda.

Settling back into her seat, with her back against the warm worn wood of her shed and her face turned up towards the sun, she reflected again how much she loved this little plot of land and all that it stood for in her life. A little piece of peace, a haven from all of the hustle and bustle of daily life. On the whole she liked the people and their quaint quirky ways. She liked the camaraderie and the support they had given her when she had arrived four years ago. How they had pitched in with seeds, advice and help. They kept an eye out for each other and helped when it was needed. They were all reeling from the run of bad luck that had hit the allotments this year and often little groups would gather to swap gossip and give advice on protecting their produce.

With a sigh, she began to review her allotment. Everything was doing well. Rain had come at the right time and sunshine had warmed the earth just in time for an early planting season. Everything was lush and ripening and tasty. It just deserved to be recognised for once. Just for once she wanted to beat the Judging Committee.

Her attention was caught by her runner beans. They were looking healthy, long and straight. Definitely worthy of a prize. Across the way stood Bill the Beans's beans. Straight and long – probably not a patch on hers but prize-winners for the last six years.

Carefully Linda looked about her. Bill's water butt stood beside his shed and the lid lay next to it. It would be just a moment's work to walk past it to the compost heap and empty something – the remainder of the Weedol – into the water as she passed. After all, all was fair in love and vegetable growing.

Before she could think about it she was up. Clutching a pile of courgette leaves in one hand and the open bottle of Weedol hidden beneath it, she quickly headed to the compost heap. As she drew level with the water butt she poured the liquid in under the pretence of shifting her burden. Luckily there was no one around now but she had to be careful. Then she dumped the leaves and returned to her seat to eat her lunch.

Later that afternoon Bill returned. He brought a piece of his wife's fruit cake and they shared it with some fresh tea. They never talked much – the allotment holders weren't always big on chat but Linda liked Bill's company and his wife's cake was definitely the best she had tasted. Idly she wondered why she didn't enter the cake competition. Then her phone rang.

Usually she left it off when she was up at the allotment but her mother had had a funny turn at the weekend and she felt that she might be needed. Sure enough it was her mother in a panic about something – she was too upset to make herself clear. Linda stood up, shaking cake crumbs from her shirt.

"Mother," she said.

Bill nodded his understanding. "You'd better go, maid. Don't worry about locking stuff up – I'll do that for you."

"You're a gem, Bill," she said as she mounted her bicycle and began to peddle home.

Later, after she had found her mother's missing spectacles – yes, that had been the crisis – she was putting a rubbish bag in the bin as Bill trudged up the hill towards his cottage across the street.

"All okay?" he called as he passed.

"Fine," answered Linda. "Another mole hill."

"I locked up for you, lass. Oh, and your plot was looking a bit dry after all the sunshine today so I gave it a drop a water – no trouble like. Your butt was looking a bit dry too so I used water from mine - save dragging it over to the tap. See you tomorrow, lass. Looks like it's going to be another grand day."

Linda let the dustbin lid drop with a clatter and turned sadly towards the house. At least no one could suspect her of being the culprit now, and there was always next year.

Walls

Abby Williams

She wanted clean walls
Bare walls
Walls under control
"Mizzle", "Drizzle", "Dulux White" -
Walls with little
Soul

No scraps of paper
blu-tack scars
No painted butterfly hands
No air-dried clay
or sellotape or
collaged rubber bands

She wanted empty halls
No shoes left out
No schoolbags in the way
Cupboards free from
Fingerprints
Remotes lined up on their tray

She wanted peace
No arguments
The milk put away
Beds made for visitors
who never came
to stay

She smuggled paintings
Crayonwork
softly to the bin
Cardboard cows
and dinosaurs
They all
went
in

She wanted roasted peppers
and chickpeas
with "bits"
And eating-with-mouths-closed
and no more
nits

She pickled words and
made them sour
and showered them around
Until they put their
shoes away without
making a
sound

And now they've gone.
Her walls are bare
They stare blank
as the moon
They're painted in "Regret"
and
"Wished Away Too Soon"

Beached

Abby Williams

The beach is nearly empty. It is only the horse riders and dog walkers who shoulder the bleached morning sky. And me, of course. The sand is damp and dark, shaded by the sullen cliffs. The sea is slate grey, laced in white.

I shiver and zip my hoodie up to my chin. The surf shack and café and toilets are shuttered. The lifeguards' abandoned tower, feet buried, rises skeletally, alien, post-apocalyptic in the grey light. It is hard to imagine that in a few hours the sun will dance in the sky, and children, zigzagging to the water, will kick sand onto strangers' towels. Clockfinger bodies will mark out the hours as they track the orbiting sun, and sweating ice-creams will slide off cones. But not yet.

I make my way down the dunes, the stiff sea grasses scratching at my bare legs. My toes in their sliders are cold.

I aim for the lifeguards' tower. This is my spot. Today is Wednesday so Oisín will be on duty. It's pronounced 'Uh-sheen.' Isn't that beautiful? Like water dragging out over pebbles. Oisín is a student of business management at Exeter. During term-time he works at the gym on campus – when he can get the shifts. But in summer he comes here, to the coast, for the surfing.

I grapple with my shorts. They are surf shorts. New. I wasn't sure about them. In the shop mirror I gazed at the acres of white thigh, pitted with tiny flesh craters, and I grimaced at the assistant.

"I don't know..."

"Be brave!" she said, flicking her ponytail over her shoulder, as she went to tidy the sunglasses. "They look cute." Cute.

She had had her back to me as she said it. Her shoulder blades stood out like fairy wings, and she wore a spaghetti strap vest with no bra. The shorts bit into the soft mallow of my belly, anticipating waist. But Penny's voice echoed in my ear.

"Don't put yourself down. Be positive. Be kind to yourself."

Were surf shorts kind? I pushed my glasses up my nose. On balance, I decided to buy them. Maybe I was being overly critical of myself. Maybe my thighs weren't so vast.

Here on the beach, they are difficult to get off. I can barely get my thumbs in the waistband and as I inch them downwards they graze my skin. It is like being peeled. I would have got the next size up, but they don't make one. I unzip my hoodie, drop it on top of my sliders. I pull the glasses from my face and drop them on top of the hoodie. Immediately the world is blurry, my body a pale amorphous mass. It makes it easier to go in. To plunge into that concrete-grey sea. I stretch and walk towards the water. This is the worst bit. I feel more than naked. Like every part of my skin is under a microscope. My swimming costume cups and bulges, breasts indeterminable from other slab rolls. *Be kind to yourself.* When the water is just above my knees I plunge towards invisibility. The cold sucks the air from my lungs. It is like a punch and I gasp. Just move. Move, move, move. I force breaths in and out and soon I am too numb to feel anything.

I have been doing this swim for three weeks now. It's part of my self-care routine. Because Penny says body and mind are connected. If you improve one it bounces back on the other and before you know it you've stopped spending the day café-hopping and buying kitchenware, trying to post envy-inspiring selfies from just the right angle to create the illusion of single-chinnedness, and you have a full and meaningful life. With Oisín.

God, did I think that out loud? I didn't mean it.

He'll be here at 9.30. The waves flick up and salt-lick my cheeks. It is fresher today. Back on shore the café man is battling with his bunting. The wind tugs on it like a puppy.

There are some big rollers out here. I feel them lift and rock me like a mother's arms. I am weightless and wonderful. I am a clipper, carving through the water, and I could swim forever. But when I finally cruise into the shallows, feeling the sand grate my belly, and I stagger to my feet, I find my legs are not my legs but slow-setting cement. *Be kind to yourself. Don't overdo it.*

Oisín is kind. He is forever having mums come up to him with panic-stricken children dangling from their arms asking where the toilets are, and he never loses his patience, even though there is literally a sign pinned to the lifeguards' station: 'Toilets' and an arrow. He's really relaxed. He's a gamer too. He noticed my Princess Zelda t-shirt. I mean, most people don't even see me, let alone read my t-shirt. I fantasise sometimes about Oisín and cosplay. He would make an *amazing* Jon Snow.

I emerge from the water. My hair is dark seaweed, my skin mottled pink. I dry myself off with my grey-white bath towel and arrange my *Game of Thrones* beach towel neatly on the sand. The loos aren't open yet so I have to do elaborate things with t-shirts and bra clasps, my towel trying to escape from my damp grip. The keen ones are starting to arrive now. By the time the beach is in full sun I will be dressed, with detangled hair and lathered in sun lotion. Once it's on, I don't have to reapply it. I hate people watching me rub it in.

The sun is higher now. It's funny. You read your book for half an hour, look up, and the beach has gone from deserted to busy to crammed. I sit at the feet of the lifeguard tower. I am not worshipping him or anything! It's just that my skin is so pale that I prefer to sit in the shadows. Oisín arrived about an hour ago. He did the *Star Trek* salute at me. He's hilarious. I love it that we have these private jokes.

Of course, *she's* here too. "Billie". I don't know if that's her name, that's what I call her because she's like a skater-chick-tortured-soul kind of girl à la Billie Eilish.

She's so wrong for him. I mean, he wants someone more natural, more real. But she still turns up, every day about ten. It's embarrassing. She's always finding reasons to talk to him. "Oisín, do you think it'll rain today?" "Oisín have you heard the latest Echosmith album?" I mean, please. Can't she see he's not interested? I read my book. It's good to know that I'm not the most desperate girl on the beach. But sometimes she *does* make him laugh. Maybe he likes her after all. Maybe I should try a little harder? I munch on a cereal bar. It is like eating hard-baked cat litter.

The sun is hot still but the wind has got stronger. It's the kind of wind that whips the heat out of summer so you don't realise you're burning until you get home and you find your shoulders are raw and you are still wearing a skin-white swimsuit. A parasol bounces across the sand in front of me, a red-faced dad in falling-down cargo shorts chases after it. Oisín's radio sputters and he talks into it, then creaks down the steps to his tower and walks out to the water. His calf muscles flex under his brown skin. In the distance, a tiny Oisín unfurls the red flags. I look at the water. The surf has swelled. Like a crowd of lads in a bank-holiday beer garden, it has got full of itself, it is teetering towards danger. I'm glad I got my swim in early.

I can't believe it. It's a long walk from one end of the beach to the other. I am too busy watching the waves to notice that Billie – sneaky Billie – has nipped to the café and is walking towards him with two polystyrene cups. Well now he'll *have* to talk to her. Just to be nice. In fairness, that was a pretty clever move. Respect, Billie. She is chattering away, but his attention flickers between her and the sea. There are small children at the water's edge, jumping over the surf. Finally one of their mums comes and grabs an arm, gesturing at the flags, and the rest limp along behind her like a windless kite. Now he gives her his full attention.

When they get back to the tower she sits down next to him. On the steps. And he doesn't tell her to get off. In fact, he is chatting to her about surfing, about the thrill of catching the wave and she is banging on about skateboarding, somebody called Ollie. If that girl can skateboard my mum can kite-surf. I can't believe he is falling for this.

"I didn't know you could ride?"

"Yeah, I mean I'm not great, but I love it. I'd love to try surfing one day."

Oh. *Purlease.* In a way, it's annoying, because maybe this means that Oisín isn't actually too bright after all. Or it means he is really genuinely kind and lovely to people. So maybe he is just being kind and lovely when he talks to me.

This thought sits in my belly like a stone. Suddenly the beach feels suffocating. The salt is stiff in my hair, my thighs chafe against each other in these stupid shorts and the smell of suntan lotion is nauseating. And the noise. Kids squealing. Phones beeping. And always, always, Billie's tinkling laugh and Oisín's warm voice. It is unbearable. It is like my skin is contracting, my insides are itching. I feel like I am going to burst or vomit or pass out. I leap up.

"Oh my God!"

In my ears my voice is loud. But nobody else hears. Nothing

stops. I say it again, shriller, louder.

"Oh my God!"

And now Billie and Oisín both look round, Billie with a sucking-lemons mouth, but Oisín's expression is curious, mildly alarmed. I raise my arm, my doughy finger pointing.

"Out there."

Now they both shade their eyes with cupped hands. Oisín finally remembers his binoculars – lifeguard yellow to match his t-shirt – and raises them.

"I can't – I can't see anything."

I point again, more urgently.

"Out there. It's a boy. I think it's a boy. I think he's in trouble."

Oisín bites his lip. His brow is furrowed. He has freckles all across his nose. He suddenly looks young. Billie's eyes are wide.

"Jesus," she whispers, and she looks between Oisín and the maybe-boy in the sea, excitement tugging her mouth corners. In her mind, she is probably already tweeting about it.

I wonder if he's going to do it. I mean – he *is* here to work, not to flirt. There could well be a boy out there, a poor child out of his depth. I look at him with cold-boulder eyes and my mum's best, 'And what are you going to do about it?' face. He grabs the inflatable from the side of the hut and sprints towards the water, straddling the incoming surf and now plunging into the waves.

I feel proud of him. As if he is somehow connected to me. He has gone into the sea at my bidding. I slide a look across at Billie – "See?" – but she is watching the waves. Oisín is so small next to those rolling monsters. It takes forever for him to travel up one steep side, and then he disappears from sight, in the hammock between waves.

I want to call him back. It might have been a seal, I want to say. I just wanted it to stop. Them to stop. But he is crawling through the water now, diving under the avalanche mountains, and now he is a little dot, his dark hair almost impossible to pick out in the grey-sky seas. Suddenly he disappears. He was there, and now he's gone.

We watch and watch, Billie and I, hanging on the tails of the same breath as if we've used up all the air in the world. Finally he pops up again and a small happy "oh" escapes Billie's goth-black lips. We see a flash of white moon face turned beach-ward for a fraction of a second. And then there is just sea.

I am sand-shackled, frozen. We wait for him to pop back up. He did before. I mean, Oisín is a strong swimmer. He wouldn't have gone if it was too dangerous. Would he? *Would* he? And we wait. And we wait. But this time he does not pop back up.

"It could have been a seal," I whisper.

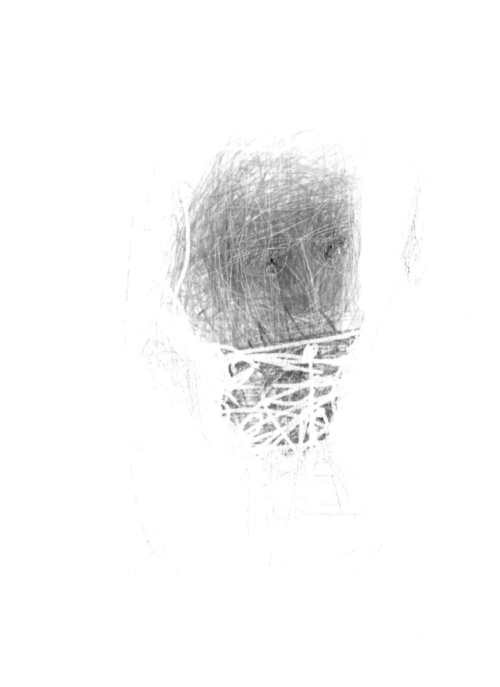

Back to Water

Wendy Watkins

The internet can't catch everything.
You can go fishing for a name
but it's like following
tadpole tracks.

You can't know everything.
What's gone is gone
and the stranger who trembled like
a mouse for a day needs to run
back to the wild.

Sometimes you need to
leave names behind,
let ink dry in the inkwell,
put down your pen.

Walk backwards,
not knowing,
nameless,
where the wild mind lives.
Let what is gone go back to water.

Untitled

Wendy Watkins

A chocolate truffle
is a zen poem
melting
on the tongue,

a cormorant
opening sweet dark wings
into the sky of your body.

Temple

Wendy Watkins

The shortest distance
between
sacred listeners
is the stethoscope

suspended gently,
like a black-corded
Tingsha-chime.

One disc
held softly
to the heart,
the other
presses lightly
against
the listening
for that
crimson sound –
the temple door
within her –

opening,
closing,
opening.

The Physician
and the
Suffering One
together
inside
the listening,

wordless,
lemniscating,
within the
ancient hum
of temple bees.

Whittling

Anna Hattersley

To avoid accusations of idleness, I whittle beneath the large chestnut on the green for as long as my weary fingers will allow. Then I sheath my knife and, as I watch the autumn leaves fall, I remember my first nickname; Zig.

Zig was forever climbing trees, brandishing enormous sticks and battling monstrous pirates on the high seas. After one particularly bloody battle, my mother said I was lucky not to have lost an eye. She called me names that I had never heard before and was told never to repeat. The scar is still there, although she is not.

Tuesday Weekes. Yes, Tuesday as in the day of the week and Weekes, W-E-E-K-E-S. What fair and considerate person would give a four-year-old so many 'e's to contend with? How I yearned to be Kate Smith and trample on Tuesday Weekes with my wellingtons.

Tuesday Poos-day. Wee-wee Weekes. Children are cruel, but so are parents when they name us so lightly. Why can I still not shed these names and be free?

JD heart TW. The rough, jagged initials you scratched in the oak tree by the goal posts remain, but I would not recognize JD today.

T.T, Weeksey, Number 10. Names from when I was fit, strong, outgoing. No one has uttered them in decades. Did they fall to the ground and rot?

Ruby Tuesday, Dr Weekes, my love, Mummy, Mum, Nanna. These names are not faded, crumpled leaves I want to shed.

When winter storms shake my boughs, I will relinquish not one of them. My names are deep within me. They are the rings of my tree.

So, do not accuse me of idleness for this is my ultimate work. I gently wiggle my knife from its leather sheath and carve.

Paper Knickers

Julie Mullen

When I'm eighty-five I won't be wearing a bra
or paper knickers
I will Jack-knife myself into short
black cocktail dresses
show my arms to all and sundry
dare to confide in someone's
someone about someone
I will snog the moon
ravage the sun
smooch with stars
wear big wigs powder pink
give Dame Edna a run for her money
I will refuse to be photoshopped or
airbrushed when appearing in
The Dartmouth Gazette for my outrageous
performance poetry *@Dartingtonhashtagoldbat*
@wow@sinkinghearts@someonesaunty
@hasntgotaclueshesawful@sadoldsad
@getheroffstage
I will urinate in bins to show bins that I can
outclimb any vine from Sharpham
I will wear elaborate jewellery fighting off
armed robbers and those without alms
I will have all the political opinions and be
an everyman for herself
I won't eat for days and when I do it will only be

certain foods of a certain colour
most of all I will deliver kindness through silly letterboxes
true kindness I only ever fantasised about
I will be the biggest philanthropist
known to man known to woman
going commando into the infinity
drumming in the
night on a Totnes high street
with juvenile delinquency emblazoned
burning bright into a possum of curiosity.

Torniquet Dad

Julie Mullen

It's funny what you remember
in the house of better days -
mum with her fruit bowl smile
her bashing a spider
"the roadkill" of the bathtub.

Mum a bra-full of brazen gravitas
telling us that she was frozen
in this house -
had peas up her bosom
beauties she said oh and
that nipples made a difference.

We were always reading between
her lines and that was before dementia.

I remember dad only as a torniquet
at dinner without napkin.

Parents both trying desperately to keep it cheap.
Us kids with a tangerine tambourine.

In the 60s, replicating Beatles smiles
And screams and smirks and hair
watching our peas and queues.
Deadman-dad of the pub, his
three sandwiches
short of a spider picnic
convalescing in his kids dreams
brandishing our own reality.

Stations of the Cross

Julie Mullen

Part I

Never take sweets from a man with a hernia for a face,
Everyone knows that.
A jackdaw pecking car, curb crawling in an effortless,
bang in the bonnet affordable Zephyr
With protracted portholes.
It's a screamer. I name him widows windows.
Welcome to my 1965 Easter sunshine diary.

Part II

It's a bad Friday for me, a child of 7.
I am 7. 6th child of 6, in Liverpool.
It is 2 o'clock in the afternoon.
My sister has promised our mother 'promises'
She cannot keep:
To walk with me in blistering-sistering
Sunshine but this sister is unreliable.
A seething sibling with mob mentality
- throws me off scent for thruppence.
"You go to the shops, buy sweets," she sings.
"I will see my good friends. Ok?
"Look threepence."

Part III

I am all paralysed infamy – I take it, the coin.

Part IV

Before me, a huge road with traffic lights.
I love traffic lights. The bright lights of childhood.
The colours. My mind is all flooded
With Red, Green and Orange confusion.

Part V

I cross. No, better not.
I cross. No, better not.
I am on the cross – I've crossed.
Ball-breaker for seven.
I was five two years ago.
A major road with lights.
I'm feeling taller
for seven.
I seem to know
What I'm doing,
"Out my way, you dirty daleks."
But there aren't any daleks.
Nobody is loitering with intent.
Planet life is empty in Liverpool.

Part VI

I am the small one heading towards the shops for my sins.
2 o'clock in the afternoon for a
Playful child
(Run-away child).

Part VII

"Run-away child!"
The old mouth of wisdom says.
The soothsayer of doom is here.
Her, on spit and seclusion, in raised allegros, with throttle-veined
voice:
"Excuse me – Hernia Face –
"Is there some confusion about your protrusion?
"Is it, would you say,
"At the exclusion of all your hand-beckoning,
"Seat-warming subterfuge towards that minor?"

Part VIII

I've been told by my mother:
Never accept sweets from strangers.
I love lollipops
But I am not getting in your car for one.
I have a small threepenny bit in my hand
Clutching it I am, dreaming of big gobs full of
Fruit Salads, Swizzels and Chewits,
Oh and chocolate mice.
Of mice and men
I definitely choose mice.

Part IX

I am All
Confusion and punctured tyres for eyes,
Ears, mouth, legs.
Punishing protrusion is beckoning me to his car.

He stops three times,
Three times he stops,
Desperate to get me in his car.
Good Friday at 7
I am running
Inside I am screaming
I am running, running
Inside I am screaming
It's the man,
The man my mother
Has warned me against,
The man with sweets.

X

As chance would have it
I run into the arms of
A mother with her daughter
Walking a dog –
The man in the Zephyr
Hernia Face, pretends
He has not a care in the world,
Stops for cigarettes from the
Old vending machine
My eyes are full of tears,
Thin white skittle legs shaking,
The thruppence in my pocket
Shelters in a foreign pocket
Of relief.

XI

Three days later in Birkenhead

XII

A poor child is found murdered

XIII

A photofit of "Hernia Face" turns

XIV

The obverse and the reverse of
My coin to dim.

The Primrose Macbeth Stories

Julie Mullen

Writers and playwrights litter the streets of Bloomsbury, or so it is claimed. At least one man walked past me with an absurd gait, his silk jacket soaked in self-importance and pomp. But were all these good people of Bloomsbury really famous writers dedicated to making it? Oughtn't they to be at their desk, hurriedly flinging more words at the typewriter, devising a new play or finishing their novel, sending off a poem to *The New York Times*?

They say writer's block passes but it had been three months since I had sat at my desk. This was when I began to write to her, to Agatha Christie.

Dear Agatha

I have just finished Who Killed Roger Ackroyd. *What a masterpiece. I love the way you completely hoodwink the reader. I would never have guessed it was the…. How do you do it?*

Warmest regards,

Primrose MacBeth

My first letter was sent to Agatha Christie in the autumn of 1967. I was just about to be nineteen. My aunt had told me about her summer house in Devon and I addressed all correspondence to Agatha Christie, The Summer House, Greenway, Devon. I wrote again in '68, '69 and one final letter in 1970. I never received any replies. Just before the last letter, I booked a holiday with my friend Minnie Boyd.

I was twenty-three, Minnie considerably older, a bold thirty. I had met Minnie at "The Troubadour" in London at a poetry night. We enthused about "The Liverpool Poets" over a black coffee and Minnie disclosed she had met Adrian Henri and he'd made a pass at her. Adrian Henri was crestfallen on learning she batted for the other side. She booked our accommodation in Devon. I was thrilled. Thrilled as our Paddington train sped to the land of green fields and cow manure.

We were dropped off by the Exeter bus at Dartmouth Harbour with our small nut-brown suitcases. It was 3pm and a taxi was waiting to take us to our B&B, 'Sunnydale.' We got quite a shock when we arrived at the house. There was a woman sitting on the veranda absolutely sozzled. She slurred all the way through her welcome speech telling us her name was "Moreween", guiding us to our room. Much to my horror we had been given twin beds. I was under the impression I was getting my own room but Minnie explained she was genuinely scared of sleeping alone on holidays.

The landlady amused us, late 40s, jarring red lipstick and a dreadful sickly smell of 4711 perfume, as she explained about breakfast. "It's very much help yourself to eggs and bacon and first up is in charge of cooking it."

Minnie listened, astonished, open-mouthed. Moreween went on to say she kept late hours and never normally got up before 12 noon. There was a half dead cat in a basket in the breakfast room with a nasty furball next to it. "That's Rodney, bless his heart."

Our room had a nice view of Dartmouth Harbour so we were pleased, but the sheets had a faint whiff of cigarette smoke; we made do. Minnie and I piled on cardigans, packed our notebooks and pens and dashed off to catch the remainder of the day. A key was flung out of the front door after us.

"Here, I don't want you waking me up," Moreween chirped with her happy-go-lucky landlady of the B&B smile. I think she was sobering up and needed a bit more gin.

Minnie and I walked along smiling to ourselves, so pleased with our fresh new holiday. We had a bite to eat at a greasy spoon then walked along the quay. There was a cruise boat boarding as we got there. That's when the cheery man with the blue cap made my day: "Stunning views of Dartmouth, a chance to see the whole of the River Dart estuary and glimpse the summer house belonging to Agatha Christie …"

He had said the magic words, Agatha Christie. We immediately bought tickets for the boat and climbed aboard to find it crammed with tourists with cameras, some Americans, who seemed to make the loudest noise. "Agatha Christie? Gee …"

I began telling Minnie about all my letters to Agatha Christie and my hope of meeting her on this trip. Minnie castigated me a little, saying writers need privacy and it was highly unlikely she would respond to notes, even a hand-delivered one. I must have looked disappointed because that's when the man wearing the jolly blue sailor's cap tapped me on the shoulder.

"Hey, miss," he said. "I have to get off at Greenway and deliver some shopping to Mrs Christie, do you want to help me with the bags when we land? Oh, by the way I am Teddy, Teddy Gasgoine. I couldn't help overhearing you telling the story about the unanswered letters."

I was horrified he'd heard. I had never told that story before and it was only because I really trusted Minnie that I revealed myself. I looked at Minnie's face: she lit up, laughing. I said, "Can I bring my friend?" badgering him like a skittish moorland pony.

Minnie quickly intervened, "No, I want to see Totnes. I'll stay onboard and meet you back at Sunnydale."

She was very convincing, so when we landed at Greenway, I grabbed a bag from Teddy which had 'Harrod's' scribbled in gold leaf. Teddy talked forty to the dozen and I had difficulty keeping up. My heart was thumping with frightened anticipation. We made our way to the house and Teddy pulled the bell. A girl came to the door but it wasn't Agatha, I think it was her PA. She was very dowdy and plain-faced with a fresh crop of pimples on her chin which were all inflamed. She looked about eighteen. She took the bags and Teddy gave her a whopping big smile. "I normally see Thelma the cook, is she about?"

The young girl looked peeved, "I'll go and see," she pouted. We heard her shouting, "cook, cook" as she clattered down the cobbled stairs to the kitchen.

I was losing my nerve and I was just about to bolt when Teddy caught sight of Thelma. "Hello again, are we okay for a cup of tea?"

Thelma gave Teddy a very big smile and nodded enthusiastically.

"I'm ..." Teddy interrupted, "Sorry, this is Primrose, Primrose MacBeth."

Thelma's ears perked up. "What a wonderful name, I hope you're a writer?"

I felt very sheepish. How could I declare myself a writer in this echo chamber of a hall? How dare I ... but I did! I liked the words that tumbled joyfully out of my mouth. We were led to the kitchen and given tea and biscuits, homemade biscuits made with clotted cream: one of *HER* favourite recipes. Teddy and Thelma chatted about mutual acquaintances in Dartmouth. I think they felt something for each other. She gave me a few intrigued looks.

That's when Teddy blurted it all out about my letters. More blushing from me. "Would Primrose be able to meet Agatha?"

Thelma spoke out quite firmly: "She's very private, miss. I would love to say I could get you an introduction but I would lose my job." I felt a sense of devastation flood through me.

"Thelma, how about I show Primrose the gardens – oh and the pool, the wonderful bathing house you showed me?" Before I knew what was happening, Teddy had grabbed my hand and my half-eaten biscuit fell on the floor as he dragged me off down into the gardens.

It was utterly beautiful and I just wanted to sit down with my pencil and draft a poem or a short story. He knew so much about her life; details I had never heard before. It was as though he was reading my mind because before I could say "Bingo Dandy" he had parked me on a bench with a lofty view of the River Dart.

"Sit here, you can pretend to *be* her." He headed off back to the house, telling me he would be back in half an hour.

My pencil slightly quivered and then words just fell out of me. I scribbled and scribbled. I buttoned up my cardigan (I was clearly feeling the chill from the river). I wanted to explore but I had promised not to move from the seat. Surely he wouldn't mind if I went in search of her private bathing house? I had read about her house and seen photographs of the pool, built right into the rocks. I took a risk and headed towards the water. There it was, the bathing house. "I wonder if she bathes naked," I giggled to myself. Agatha Christie in the buff, that would be an amusing story for Minnie!

I tried the door but it was locked. I peered through the windows: it was a tidal pool and was filling up. Boats passed me, gently meandering down the Dart, carelessly frolicking with a gusty motion. I popped my sunglasses on, trying to look like one of the 'Christie set'. I wondered how Minnie was, I wished she had come with me. I heard voices, very jolly voices; it was the PA, now wearing shorts, accompanied by a young man.

"What are you doing here?!" she shouted. "Have you permission?"

My mouth couldn't form any words. The young man tut-tutted at me in a spiteful manner. "Go, do you hear. Go back to the boat you came on and disappear!"

I ran away from them crying. Everything was spoiled: my stupidity taking advantage of the situation, my absurd writer's curiosity, and I blubbed all the way back to the house.

The kitchen door was locked and I began to panic. I went around to the front door in the hope of meeting Thelma or Teddy but all I heard was the faint sound of a piano being played. The house was large, Georgian and enviably grand. My tears had stopped now as I tiptoed with trepidation, drawn by the music. I pressed my face right up against the window and there she was, Agatha Christie, playing the piano. I was immediately struck by her natural grandiosity and poise. She hadn't noticed me. She was singing to an old tune that I recognised and I observed that she was crying as she sang. Just then she stopped playing and dabbed her eyes.

She looked so vulnerable. Honestly, I don't know what possessed me but I knocked gently on the window; me, Primrose MacBeth, known for being excessively weedy in most circumstances … I knocked. The world stood still, then Agatha Christie opened the French windows.

"Hello," she said. "You gave me quite a shock. Are you Lorna's friend?" Agatha must have meant the girl with the spots and the venomous tongue.

"No, I am Primrose MacBeth. I'm a writer too," I blurted out. That's all I said. My name. I didn't say what I was doing or why I was there.

"Come in, Primrose. So where have you come from?

It all came spilling out of me: how I had written to her for many years but never received any replies, but undeterred I made a pact with myself to meet the famous author.

"My dear, you are quite fearless! Most people wouldn't have dared knock on my window. Can I offer you tea?"

"No thank you," I said politely, aware that I had already eaten two of her biscuits.

That's when she did a queer thing. She took hold of my hand and led me to a cellar, flipping a light on. "I want to show you something."

I was acutely aware that the mistress of murder and deceit was in charge now. We took some stairs and there before me was a room filled to the ceiling with post. So much post. Simply letters galore. "Goodness," I gasped.

"This, my dear, is all my fan mail but I just cannot bring myself to open any of them." I asked her why and she looked acutely embarrassed. "I am too scared to face these good people who have taken their time to write to me. I just don't have answers for them. Most want clues to how I work, why I'm so successful. I'm sorry, dear, but I'm afraid your letters must be somewhere in that pile."

I noticed a tear course down her face so I proffered one of my hand-embroidered hankies that I always keep in reserve and she took it with grace. "Tell me, Primrose, when I failed to respond, how did it make you feel? Tell the truth, dear, I must know."

"Agatha, I was sad, very sad. I just kept writing anyway but this holiday was all about meeting you." We returned to the music room.

"I am so delighted to make your acquaintance. A writer's life can be intolerably lonely, you know." Agatha asked me to take a seat. She began to scribble something on her exquisite, personalised stationery. "Here," she said. "Forgive the brevity of this missive." She gently slid the paper into an envelope and I saw her gold italic pen printing my name on the front. She put her hand on my shoulder and then it happened, the moment I will never forget and will cherish for the rest of my life. She looked into my eyes and said, "Never give up, Primrose. Keep on writing."

I left the music room as she took a seat back at the piano. She trusted me to find the front door and leave. She trusted me. I walked down to the quay in a haze to look for Teddy. There was no sign of him or anyone, just a lone boat moored alongside the quay. A man came out of a hut.

"Where do you want to go, miss? Dartmouth? It's a shilling to Dartmouth."

I smiled, "I'll pay you ten, my good fellow."

I sat on the boat and began to write. It was as if she had given me a magic pen. My first book was published in 1972 as a direct result of meeting Agatha Christie. Primrose MacBeth rose to fame. The letter? Oh, I am sworn to secrecy. I can't breathe a word of what it contained, you'll just have to imagine.

Pattern

Ann Pelletier-Topping

What if my root pattern is wrong?
Is it sane to reiterate a rage
if I've known all along

I wasn't born to belong
to that self-replicating cage
because my root pattern is wrong?

Would you go on and on, all day long
sprouting never-ending loops of shame
if you've known all along

and all you've done is prolong
fractal chaos, all-out rampage
because your root pattern is wrong?

Cut here,
        the wise one said. Don't pass on
your heinous streak that amplifies with age.
Deep down you've known all along

you must do more than just leave. So go on,
face the storm, find a better landing stage
because your root pattern is wrong
and you've known all along.

Granddaughter Moves In

Ann Pelletier-Topping

The grandma's purple leg is full of flesh-
eating-maggot holes. Each morning she hammers
her hip into gear, limps past the old gas
furnace and makes breakfast. After the dishes
are tidied away, she sits on her chair
and chains her leg to it. All day long she looks

out the window while her cuttings in old jars look
vibrant and grow roots, on the sill. The purple flesh
she got by falling off a ladder, not off a chair,
as some rumoured, broke her hip as she hammered
on a curtain pole while good-for-nothing Grandad ate dishes
of peanuts in the corner tavern and gassed

about imagined war wounds instead of buying gas
as promised. But the grandfather never looks
unshaven and though he won't help with the dishes,
he'll bounce the grandchild on his knees, making the flesh
around his neck wobble a bit. By teatime he's hammered
on London Dry and falls asleep on a chair,

bless him. He doesn't like being tied to his chair
and usually disappears off behind the town's gas
works for most of the week, before the grandma hammers
out his tedious list of chores. What he looks
for, rumour has it, are the sinful pleasures of the flesh,
but who could blame him with a wife who dishes

out abuse at him, worse than the priest dishes
out his penance. The granddaughter, on her plastic chair,
undresses her doll and doodles on its pink flesh,
You bad baby, you only good for the gas
chamber. She throws it behind the furnace and looks
at the grandmother. Picking up her doll, she hammers

its head on the floor. *You hurt? Won't hammer*
you no more. She puts pretend dishes
on the table for tea, feeds her baby. *Look,*
Grandad coming up the stairs. He sits on the chair
to take off his rubber galoshes. *Where's the gas!*
says the grandmother, wanting her pound of flesh.

You useless piece of flesh, she lays into him like a hammer
then the gas runs out with a pshhh. *Cakes?* says the child,
dishing
them out, him on the chair, her giving him the look.

The Birthday Present

Ruth Brooks

"Oh no, not again!" I yelp, sucking my thumb and hopping round the workshop.

I've hammered myself, instead of the nail – for the fourth time in the last hour. I swear, a very rude word, but under my breath. Mum forbids us to swear. It's un-Godly and He would be very angry.

I feel tears prickle my eyes. I am useless. A disgrace to my family. But I have to stop the huge sobs bursting out of me. Otherwise Mum'll hear me. I must keep what I'm doing a secret. I take ten deep breaths. Luckily Mum's indoors, busy baking bread. The warm, crusty smell wafts out of the open door.

I creep across the yard, just to check. The wind is up, blowing the sandy, dry soil down from the scrubby hills. It mixes with the dust and straw and earth on the ground. I peep round the door. Mum is kneading another batch of dough. Next to her, my little sister Rachel is carefully shaping her own little ball into animals. Baby Sarah sleeps soundly in her cradle under the eaves of the staircase. Mum's face is flushed, strands of her long black hair damp and clinging to her forehead. She's got that kind of expectant, excited look that I used to see, before Jay left home and all the worry started, before her face became sad and thoughtful. But today she's happy, because tomorrow afternoon, not only is it Rachel's birthday, but also, praise to God, Jay's coming home on one of his rare visits.

I heave a sigh of relief that Mum's otherwise occupied. I hate it when I'm trying to do something and it's all going wrong and Mum, with her sharp eyes, notices and fusses. It makes her hover. I get jittery when she hovers, her face a mixture of worry and pity and sadness. And puzzlement: why am I so bad with my hands, when the rest of the family are so brilliant? My dad, a master carpenter, my three brothers set to follow in his footsteps, and Jay, my half-brother, a genius at woodwork. I'm a sad disappointment to Dad. He's always singing their praises. Sometimes he hardly bothers to look at me.

Mum tries to stick up for me. At night, I can hear them talking from my bed on the platform above the kitchen.

"Simon's only twelve, dear," she says to Dad, in her soft, patient voice. "He's still growing, and learning."

"Huh! Simple Simon, that's what he is," snorts Dad. And then he bangs on about Jay and how brilliant he was when he used to work with Dad. You'd think the sun shines out of his ar – backside. Jay left home about a year ago, and went 'a-wandering', as Mum puts it. Travelling on foot to different villages and talking to people. Teaching them stuff. Or he'd be hanging round our village, chatting to all the elders, asking them questions.

Anyway, my thumb's stopped throbbing so I'm ready to have another bash with the hammer. I had this idea, see, of making a cot for Rachel. I managed to saw the wood okay with the pieces the right size. But when I tried to put it all together, I got stuck. And now, I can't get the nails in. The sides keep collapsing. Oh, Hell. This is a disaster.

I suppose I could ask one of my brothers. But they'd look at me pityingly, and probably take over. Then it would be their present to Rachel, not mine.

In a way, though I'm a bit jealous of Jay being Mum and Dad's favourite, I do wish he was here. I'd ask him to help and he wouldn't sneer or take over. Yes, I know I made him sound a bit weird, but he has a gentle, soothing way about him. He was always kind to all of – to everyone we knew, really. Helpful. Kind of tuned-in to what people were thinking and feeling. But maybe he wouldn't have time for me now. After all, he's twenty years older than me.

Mum and Dad get all misty-eyed when they talk about him. There's some mystery there that no-one's ever explained to me. I heard my brothers talking once when they thought I was asleep. I learnt that Dad wasn't Jay's real father. That he met Mum when she had Jay in her tummy and he helped to look after her, until he was born. Then Dad went off somewhere, and it was only years later that they met up again and got married and had my brothers and me and my sisters.

If I could only hold these two pieces together, I can nail them together. What would Dad do? Ah, a clamp. If I can just prop the wood up – yes! I'm doing it! – and wind the handle... Not too tight. There. Now, get the nails and hammer ready. I've gone and hit my sodding thumb again. (Oh, forgive me, God, that was wicked). Poor thumb – it's black and blue. And the thing has fallen apart again. What to do? Breathe, breathe, deep and easy. If I stay still, God will send me the answer, that's what Jay used to tell us all. That is, if He isn't too angry with me for swearing...

Wow! God's in a good mood today. He's sent me the answer. Glue! I must glue the pieces before nailing them together. It's not here, in the workshop. If it was, it would stink the place out. But yesterday I saw Dad stirring a great mass of it in a big pot out in the yard. I hate watching him, because I feel so sorry for the poor miserable creature that had to die to provide the glue.

I've found the pot. I spread glue over the edges of two of the cot pieces, and then clamp them together. I'll do it piece by piece. The glue has to dry before I put the nails in later. I hope I don't get myself in a panicky muddle.

While I'm waiting for it to dry, I'll check up on my two donkeys, Saul and Isaac. Make sure they've got enough food and give their coats a brush. They're always pleased to see me, lumbering up to the wooden fence and braying excitedly, waiting for the treats I always bring. When I grow up, I want to work with donkeys. Mum's proud of the way I look after the goats, too – stopping them gobbling up Dad's vegetables and checking that they haven't broken through the fences. Maybe I'll be a goatherd, instead.

I love my parents, but I hate the way that they're so secretive about everything. Especially about Dad's age. I keep asking but they just laugh and tell me he's thirty-two. Well, I'm useless at number-work but even I can see that he's old enough to be my grandad – much older than Mum. I try to work it all out in my mind, and it keeps me awake at night. The latest thing that's puzzling me – worrying me, actually – is something I heard Mum saying to Dad. They thought I was asleep. But at night, on my platform above the kitchen, with my brothers snoring next to me – in that midnight in-between time, when the moon is high in the sky, and the world is silent, while Mum mends our tunics and Dad stares into the fire-flames, before the cock crows and the dogs start barking – they often murmur in low voices.

A couple of nights ago, Mum was sobbing. I crept close to the edge of the platform.

"Joe," she was saying in a choking voice, "I know that it's God's will, and whatever He decides is for the best. But this is testing my faith to the limit. Surely a loving God couldn't be so cruel?"

Dad was hugging Mum. "Hush, dearest," he was saying, "We always knew that Jay was special. God knows what is best."

Then Mum lifted her head and stared into Dad's eyes.

"I've had a premonition. A vision. I know what's going to happen to him. And it's horrible. Oh, God, please keep Jay out of danger!"

Well, by this time, I was trembling all over, and didn't sleep a wink all night.

Today, I'm up at the crack of dawn. I creep out to the workshop. To my amazement, the cot looks really good. I'd already sanded it down and varnished it. Now, I give it one last shine with a rag. I go back into the house, carrying it carefully, then place it in front of the fireplace, with Rachel's favourite doll covered with a soft cloth, inside. Silently, I climb upstairs, and wait, and watch.

Down in the kitchen, cosy in her small bed under the window, Rachel is the first to wake up. She rubs her eyes, sits up and looks around. Then she sees the cot.

"Happy birthday, little sister!" I call down to her.

By now, the whole family's awake.

"Wow!" exclaims my big brother James, "That's a nice piece of work. Who did it? Was it you, Dad?"

I hurtle down the steps, waving my arms.

"No – it was me!" I squeak and yell at the same time.

There they all are, my family, looking at me as if they've seen a ghost. Mum has tears in her eyes and even Dad gulps and swallows and gives me a half-hug.

"We'll make a carpenter of you yet, son," he says in a choking voice.

Hang on, I think to myself, *I want to be a goatherd or donkey breeder, not a carpenter.* But I don't want to upset them at such a special moment, so I keep shtum.

"He'll be more than a carpenter," says Mum, quietly, her eyes wide. "I reckon that one day he'll follow in Jay's footsteps and help to spread God's word. He'll make us all proud."

Well, it turns out to be one of those golden mornings. No one is teasing or annoying anyone else for once, and my brothers aren't arguing or fighting. Dad slips out to do some work, and Mum begins preparing the lunch – a feast fit for the king himself.

"Well, I've killed the fatted calf!" she jokes as usual. And we all laugh. Of course, we can't afford a fatted calf. But there's a chicken roasting on the spit, fresh vegetables from the garden, the delicious loaf, with its domed, brown crust, and some of her special oatmeal-and-date biscuits.

I sit down on the floor and play with the baby and Rachel, trying to keep them out of Mum's way. I always feel a bit stupid playing with dolls, but Rachel looks so happy, putting them into the new cot and singing to them and taking them out again, and I'm so proud that I've actually managed to make something out of wood which didn't fall apart, and without giving up.

Suddenly I hear voices in the yard. I spring up and look out through the open door. Dad's there, shouting, with his arms outstretched towards the figure walking slowly towards our gate. He's a tall young man, with a beard and a flowing white tunic, sandals on his feet, and a kind of turban, fastened with a band, to keep off the sun, which shines around his head, like a halo. He's smiling, looking towards our hut, waving at us.

We all run out, whooping with delight. But as I hug him, another feeling mixes with the joy, something dark and terrifying: a gnawing fear that grips my insides and makes my heart pound.

I too have a premonition: a vision of events to come, happenings too dreadful to talk about. And because of these – and I know it in my very bones – today will be the very last time that I'll see my brother Jesus.

Narwhal (monodon monoceres)

Caroline Lodge

Isn't Nature wonderful
making lion and star fish, sea snakes
and her own ocean unicorn?

Lunar whales, spears as prows,
but no purpose discovered, challenging Darwin.
Arctic giants on ice floe patrol.

Magic, fantasy, teasing, existing?
Silent swimmers, stealthy in icy seas,
studied when found, innocent of our ways.

A tooth grows long, spirals forward,
twisted ivory tusk, rare lance,
a courtier's gift to Queen Bess.

I held one once, length of my arm,
stem stained as smokers' fingers;
found with umbrellas in a friend's inheritance
sold for a house in Ireland.

Watched as wielded to combat
terror, violence, deceit, hatred,
briefly famous (London Bridge November 2019).
Isn't Nature wonderful?

From The Conchie Road

Caroline Lodge

Princetown, Dartmoor, Spring 1917

"You!" Battersby had been a warder in the prison and was used to commanding the men he supervised. He pointed at Sam. "Yes, you! You look like a strong lad. What's it to be? The road or the field?" Sam chose the road. He could work alongside Frank and the gang and they could talk politics as long as they had breath. They collected shovels and spades to move the earth, hammers to break the rocks, barrows to cart the stones and wooden mattocks to tamp down the surface.

"We're on the road to nowhere," muttered Fred as they assembled. The work detail moved off, each man keeping the one in front in sight for the Dartmoor mist had descended during the night and it was easy to lose your companions. "Keep up! Keep up!" Battersby's voice called to them from the front of the line. The men behind him had slowed, hoping he would go ahead and get lost but the group following them collided with their backs. They swore at each other until Battersby commanded them forward.

No one liked working when the mist was up. There was no mitigation, no birdsong, no view, no breeze, just the wet that got into everything. When the mist lingered for several days it became impossible to dry out work clothes in the old prison cells. Fred said that the governor knew this and had ignored the hoses that had been turned on them the week before. Sam's jacket was still wet, despite the oilcloth he had pinned to the shoulders.

"On the road to nowhere." That was Bert. "Doing work of national importance." He clapped Sam on the back. "National importance, for the bloody Prince of Wales, that's what you're doing, comrade, on the Tor Royal party!"

"Not for the nation," said Fred.

"Not for the war effort neither," said Bert.

"It's good to build a road isn't it? It might help someone – a road on Dartmoor?" Sam's companions laughed.

"Have you ever asked where this road is going from and where it's going to?" Fred was at Sam's shoulder now, speaking quietly for he had been warned about stirring up trouble. "Who benefits from a road from Princetown? And where's it going? Bloody Prince of Wales' land, that's where. And a bloke I know in Plymouth was telling me last week that the reason they haven't farmed on that Royal Field those other men are digging, the reason they haven't farmed there is that the soil won't support it. Too thin, see? So there will be no farming, and we are building a road to the place where there will be no farming. Makes you sick."

"Keeps us busy," said Bert.

"Why should the working man support the Prince of Wales?" Fred was getting worked up. "It's not national importance, it's bloody class privilege, that's what it is."

"Don't complain, Fred. We could be digging the drainage ditches."

"And why don't they use horses, bloody horses to plough the field?" Fred was off again. "Don't tell me they need them for the Front. All that digging by hand! It's just punishment, that's what it is."

Battersby had arrived at the place where the road ended and was assigning the work. He set Sam's group to level the ground.

"Give us a song, Frank," he shouted as they stepped forward into the mist.

It was a Monday morning as I have heard them say,

Our orders came from Manchester we were to march away.

Leaving many a pretty fair maid to cry whatever shall I do,

For the Lancashire lads have gone abroad, whatever shall I do?

They worked through the morning, clearing the peat and stones, the mist and wet conditions hampering their progress, soaking into their clothes. Inadequate boots were soon complained of.

"It's your conspiracy, Fred," called one of the rock crushers. "They plan for us all to have trench foot, whether we are in France or not."

The mist thickened through the morning and after their break Battersby sent them back to the work centre. Frank walked with Sam.

"How you holding up, lad?" Sam had arrived in the centre about a month earlier.

"All right. I'm used to heavy work, not like some of the others."

Frank's voice came warm and full of humour through the mist. "Read all about it! Conchies break down class barriers!" Sam laughed as the group began a discussion on class in the work camp and how things differed from 'outside'. Fred and his mates had accepted him as soon as he explained the case he had made to the tribunal and he had already attended three Socialist Club lectures and a couple of discussion groups.

Living conditions were harsh in the former prison: sleeping in the cramped cells, poor food, the eternal damp, hostility from former wardens, unrelenting work details and isolation from the world they knew. Some men had been lucky, working in the kitchens, on the farms, or in the laundry. Sam had found a group who shared his beliefs and were providing an education through their endless discussions, debates and readings. Fred called it the University of Princetown. Sam settled down for the duration.

On Sundays they were free to explore Dartmoor, to hike miles across the wild landscape, singing Socialist anthems and listening to Frank's endless repertoire of folk songs, mostly about lads and lasses. Sam went out as often as he could, despite working on the road six days a week. On that Sunday evening they had timed their return to the work centre badly. As they passed the Princetown church, the congregation emerged from evensong.

Abuse was already familiar to the men, familiar from neighbours at home, those who gathered outside the tribunals, the newspaper articles. It was familiar, but it always made Sam nauseous. On that evening it had begun with a few pebbles thrown by the boys playing in the graveyard.

"Conchies! Cowards!" they heard boys shout. And as the adults emerged they too found their voices, and the missiles and abuse increased. Fred halted his steady swinging stride, and stood, arms akimbo, facing their tormentors. This infuriated the congregation and they redoubled their barrage with uprooted weeds, rocks, and even a prayer book. Sam had been amazed to see the vicar climb onto a high stone grave and wave his arms around encouraging his flock as he roared

"COWARDS! IDOLATORS! HEATHENS! TRAITORS!"

Bile had risen in his gorge and he thought he might be sick, not with fear but disgust.

"Come on, Fred, let's go." It was Bert. "Nothing good to be done here." Frank took Sam's arm and the group stumbled up the lane towards the dark arches of the prison gates. Sam fixed his eyes on Fred and Bert's backs and his nausea receded.

They walked through the arches in silence, the pleasures of their afternoon dispersed. Fred paused and commented, "Ha! A prison is to protect people from evildoers. This one's an asylum to protect us from those evil ideas."

"Brotherhood of man," said Bert. "Bloody brotherhood of man!" Then Fred began to laugh and they clapped each other on the back and returned to their routines. Sam's nightmares began that night.

By the autumn of 1918 it was clear that the war was coming to an end but COs still arrived at the centre from the tribunals. Cases of pneumonia were identified every day and there were many who suffered from chest complaints. When Henry Haston, a recent arrival, succumbed to pneumonia the workforce gave him a good send-off, lining the route from the old prison to the railway station. Before this death the men had begun to talk about "after the war", to plan golden futures, returning to families, proper work, their homes. On that day, they lined the route singing 'Abide With Me'. Local people reminded them of the world that waited for them by throwing stones at the coffin.

[The Conchie Road appears in *Better Fetch a Chair*, a collection of short stories by Caroline Lodge.]

Underlined in Green

Barbara Childs

There they are again those green lines
Tapping on the tender membrane that is self belief,
In those dark recesses where Miss Thompson resides
Intoning – "subject predicate
      subject verb object"

I press the highlighted words.
As always it's –

    "Fragment – consider revising"

But I'm grown up now and refuse.
Don't they say poetry is like art – anything goes
And what about Haiku?
I love fragment – the word.

A drifting dandelion seed
The dissolving vapour trail in a clear blue sky
A paw print left in cement
The torn love letter
That song refrain
A new moon
Animal fur caught on barbed wire
The mud-larked old button or pottery shard

Like things half said.

"See Me" writes Miss Thompson in red
But I choose to ignore.

Felled

Barbara Childs

With one eye dark as the night
And the other blue as the sky,
Divine by birth: son of a God
His mother said.
So he thought himself invincible,
As, of course, you would.

Guided by Homer,
On the stallion Bucephalus,
He took half the known world,
From the Adriatic to the Indus,
But at thirty-two, still in his prime
When entering the gates of Babylon,

An enemy, not a rival for his empire
But another after blood,
Was lurking in the Tigris swamps.
And the ravens falling before him
Could only warn of the inevitable.

For the handsome warrior
With one eye dark as the night,
And the other blue as the sky,
Was dead within a week.

The Trench Coat

Barbara Childs

They came to learn English in summer,
but spent more time on the beach.
We loved their style, their Gallic flair.

We followed the boys on the sands,
while keeping our distance with a nonchalant air,
our catnip, the whiff of Gitanes

Longing to be like the girls -
to get the Bardot look,
we bought the trench coat but couldn't quite
carry it off, when freckled, sunburnt and gauche.

There were other rivals to contend with.
The lads had the carefree Swedes in their sights,
who knew just how to wear Le Trench.

They flipped up their collars –
belts never buckled but loosely tied,
and, as wicked rumour had it,
went commando beneath.

Maasai

Paul Skinner

The film *Out of Africa* made an indelible impression on me and when offered, I jumped at the chance of going on safari to East Africa. A friend had a part share in a rather old Land Rover allegedly left behind by the RAF when Kenya became independent. Nairobi was to be our base.

In the film Dennis Finch Hatton, the white hunter explorer, was played by Robert Redford and of course I modelled myself on him. It was to be my first trip to the Dark Continent, and I sought advice about when on safari. This turned out to be useless; "Expect the unexpected," was certainly not the advice I had expected.

After a diverted flight and a night in a Spanish hotel we arrived twenty-four hours late. Anxious to start this great adventure we loaded the old Land Rover with camping equipment, food and copious quantities of water. I wondered why so much was needed.

We headed for the Great Rift Valley and viewed the lakes Nakuru, Naivasha, and Baringo with their immense populations of flamingos, pelicans and wading birds. We travelled on towards the high escarpment forming the side of the valley and began the long ascent to the top. This proved too much for our elderly vehicle. With steam issuing from under the bonnet, our safari leader Don decided to stop to allow the Land Rover to cool and to add water from our plentiful supply.

Not being one to waste time I walked a few yards up the road with my binoculars and marvelled at the colourful small birds which occupied every bush and bit of scrub. Their names, paradise flycatcher, lilac-breasted roller, red-billed firefinch, were as exotic as their appearance.

From my high vantage point I looked at one of the wonders of the world. A geological marvel, the most extensive rift valley on earth, fifty to sixty miles wide. An ancient landscape, 25 million years in the making and still forming; two tectonic plates are moving away from each other. One day there may be two continents, two Africas.

It was peaceful with only the bird song to be heard and not a vehicle to be seen, when suddenly from out of the bushy scrub three Maasai warriors appeared, clutching spears, and started towards me along the tarmac road in a unified rhythmic swaying, rocking, trotting gait.

I knew they were Maasai, I'd seen photographs in a *National Geographic* magazine. I also knew that they drank blood and hunted lions for a hobby. The music from the film ran through my head, as the part when two formidable looking Maasai warriors also appeared from nowhere.

The three Maasai now approaching me, wore identical red robes, hanging casually off their left shoulders, ending above the knee on one side and exposing a muscular thigh on the other. The red of the robes matched their red plaited hair, and the colour extended diagonally across their faces onto their left arm. Their right arms carried a spear, held vertically with the blade uppermost. The red parts of their bodies contrasted with their brown skin; their muscles glistened with sweat in the heat of the African sun.

Curiously they wore flip-flop rubber sandals and a Kodak film canister through the extended lobe of their left ears. I wondered if perhaps that was where they kept their money? All three continued to move quickly in unison swaying rhythmically in perfect time along the road towards me.

My heart started to beat faster – what should I do? To run would be futile against these muscular looking athletes. What would Dennis Finch Hatton have done? Probably uttered some words of Swahili but I had no such skill and quickly decided to act non-chalant. I continued to casually peer through my binoculars at the colourful little birds all around me but kept one wary eye on these fearsome natives. They were now eight metres away, their rhythmic swaying, rocking gait unceasing as they drew nearer.

At three meters and without slackening pace, the spear was passed from right to left hand, the right hand was thrust forward to clutch mine and a voice in a very exaggerated English accent said "How dooo yooo doo." A second spear quickly changed hands and the same English accent said the same exaggerated words. Then the third repeat performance and they were past me, swaying, rocking, trotting still in perfect unison, down the road to where Don stood pouring water into the radiator of the Land Rover. He looked apprehensive and put down the canister of water. Then the same ritual, spear transferred, hand thrust out to grasp his, the same voice with English accent, repeated twice more and they were on their way along the road. They turned off into the bushes and were gone.

I walked towards Don, and when we met, although our mouths were open, nothing was said, there was no need. This was Africa after all.

Heaven Sent

Paul Skinner

"Oh! Thank you, thank you, our god has sent you, thank you."
The man was on his knees in front of me, hands clasped together
as if in prayer.

Have you ever wondered if God actually has an influence on
our earthly lives? I and my three companions were on safari in
Northern Kenya and had just arrived in Samburu National Park.
It was December in what is known as the short rains. The thun-
der clouds rolled across the plains in an otherwise clear blue sky.
We had just been under one of these clouds, which was like a
dozen people throwing buckets of water at the same time. Then
the sun came out and the wet ground began to steam. Fresh
green leaves glistened on the scrubby thorn bushes. Dust devils
like mini whirlwinds, were drifting aimlessly across the savan-
nah whipping up sand and dead vegetation, sending it spiralling
skywards.

It had been a difficult drive from the main gates, along a wet,
hog-backed track. It was tricky to keep the old Land Rover going
in a straight line, sliding from one side of the track to the other.
This part of the reserve was devoid of people so at least there
were no other vehicles to worry about.

We came to a low ridge and as we crested the top we were
greeted by the sight of a tourist ten-seat minibus up to its ax-
les in water, stuck in what was euphemistically called "a water
splash". Normally this would have been no more than a dry
stream bed, but the sudden downpour had awakened the stream
and brought it to life.

The native driver was giving directions from his seat in the front and all the tourist occupants were standing knee-deep in the water around the rear of the vehicle. Men, women and even the children, all trying to push the reluctant vehicle out of the brown liquid. Their clothing was the same colour as the mud-coloured porridge they were standing in. Even wide-brimmed safari hats were spattered brown. Fashionable safari suits had begun to dry in the hot sun making the group look like some sort of camouflaged military team on a mission.

I stopped the Land Rover well clear of the water and got out to view the spectacle. As soon as the driver spotted me, he jumped down from his seat and ran towards me. He landed on his knees in front of me in a muddy khaki brown heap and delightedly almost shouted at me with face turned towards the heavens, hands outstretched held together. "Oh! Thank you, thank you our god has sent you." I thought *no, mate, we just drove in through the main gates* but instead said, "Have you got a rope?"

"Yes! Yes," he said, got up and sprinted down the track, splashed into the water and opened a panel on the side of bus. He emerged clutching a wire Hauser which he clipped to the front of the bus and then to the front of the Land Rover. We returned to our driving seats, and I engaged four-wheel drive and low gear. I slowly reversed the vehicle, sceptical that anything would happen. The wire tightened and miraculously the bus started to move. Slowly it was dragged clear of the muddy porridge. The passengers cheered and a fashionable safari hat was thrown up in the air. It landed in the muddy water, where it remained. The safari trippers climbed excitedly back on the bus, the wire was removed and carefully packed away. The bus, freed from its watery prison, drew level and once again the smiling driver shouted, "thank you, thank you." Each of the bedraggled passengers waved, smiling and mouthing thank you, as the bus drove slowly past along the almost dry track and then it was out of sight. This was a safari story that would be told and retold, after dinner in the safari lodges for many weeks to come.

We were alone now, under a stunning blue African sky. I viewed the water splash with suspicion and then cautiously reversed, turned the Land Rover round and followed in the mini bus's tracks to seek more adventures.

Relearning How to Hug

Harula Ladd

Bodies, rusty and clumsy.
Hearts choke, overexcited.
How does it start again?

In the eyes. Look for
the warmth, a smile. Don't
worry, you'll recognise it.

Then raise your arms, keeping
eye contact, wrap your arms
across their back, overlapped.

Not too light or tight, don't
grab hold for dear life!
Then breathe. Now let go.

You must
let go.

Let
go.

My Taste for Rain has Changed

Harula Ladd

Too much of a good thing
the rain that came before this
spring, drenching me from sock

to soul. I longed to hang out
on the line pegged by my shoulders
arms flapping in the breeze

'til you could wring me, twist
me, squeeze me and nothing
would come out. Not a sound.

Not a drop. Then the rain
stopped. Now I'm stuck indoors
the sun mocks me, charges

at the defenceless skylight,
goads the birds I can't see but hear
into singing the raucous joys

of spring. While misery pines
for rain, permission to be
damp and heavy. Instead sun

offers a cut and blow dry, birds
catch the loosened wisps of
despair and carry them far

away like a kite lost –
When the rain comes
again I'll be ready for it.

If I were a Star

Harula Ladd

If I were a star,
which I'm not, but if I were,
I'd say:

"Turn them out! Make it darker!
Can't you see? We're trying to shine up here!
You can't make a wish on a shooting bedside lamp,
and you could do with a few of your dreams coming true.
Help us help you!"

If I were a star,
which I'm not, but if I were,
I'd say:

"Come closer, sky mates,
let's make a great galaxy,
so light and bright we could be seen
with the naked eye at night.
We'd shine so much earth folks would say,
'Wow, it's almost like it's day!
Only, in a more silvery way.'"

If I were a star,
which I'm not, but if I were,
I'd say:

"Ban all closed curtains after sundown
or you'll never know night's magic.
Curtains have their place during the day,
when the sun shines on your screens
and you can't see a thing.
But at night, it's not right to shut out the stars."

If I were a star,
which I'm not, but if I were,
I'd say:

"Remember friends, death is not our end.
The light we shone while we lived goes on
making its way toward other planets,
other galaxies, right to the edge of the universe."

If I were a star,
which I'm not, but if I were,
I'd say:

Nothing, because stars don't speak.
But they do shine, and remind us
a whole new day is just a few dreams away.

In Praise of Soil

Harula Ladd

Is it a paradox, a Pandora's box,
that more often than not hope is found
in the darkest places?
Like seeds need soil.

In a classroom once,
with a bunch of year fives,
I heard a teacher give this advice.
She held in her hands
A plastic tub of soil.

"Wash your hands after you've touched, ok?
I don't want anyone getting sick.
No touching your eyes guys.
Who knows what might be in it?"

I wanted to raise my hand and say,
"Actually, Miss, I kind of do know, in a way.
It holds life, it gives birth, to pretty much
everything that lives on earth.
It grows our food, it gives us trees,
without which, for a start, there'd be none of these."
(I'd wave a pencil in a menacing tut tut.)

But instead I held my tongue,
out of respect, perhaps misplaced,
and watched bored faces contort
into funny ugly parodies of
"Err! Gross! Yuck!"
I sighed and thought but didn't say,

Could it be education itself is leaching away
our wisdom? Like topsoil lost to heavy rains,
carried away by the rivers, because we've
stripped the land of it's fingers, grass and trees
needed to hold on to this dark, dirty majesty.

In a way that teacher was right.
We don't know what's in the soil,
until we plant a seed in it,
feed it, water it, watch it grow
into something from apparent nothing,
becoming grass, flowers, trees
then come the ants, bees, birds,
that crawl and buzz and fly,
full of life.

But it all begins with the stuff in that pot
that she told them not to touch.

The Magic Hat

Nick Nicholson

The trunk smelled of lavender, reminding me of the Yardley's atomiser, with its silk tasselled bulb that was always on my grandmothers dressing table. The leather trunk contained an accumulation of old clothes which had not seen daylight for decades. I poked through them disinterestedly sorting future rags and dusters from the stuff for Oxfam, until I suddenly recognised the hat tucked away at the bottom under some worn flannel bedsheets.

It was a brown velvet trilby, devised to be packed in a suitcase, or even a coat pocket, which could then be pushed back into shape and worn, a sort of travel hat. It had belonged to my father, though, in truth, I never saw him wear it. Perhaps it was too louche and bohemian for him, by the time I arrived. But for me, it was the entrée to so many of the imaginary adventures of my childhood.

With a little pushing and pulling I could become Jeff Arnold, a rider of the range, or by pinching the crown into a point, I was the Mountie, who always got his man. By wearing it at a different angle I turned into Alan Quartermain searching for King Solomon's mines. By pinning up one side I was a Chindit in the jungles of Burma or an Australian fighting in the Western Desert. A seagull's feather morphed me into Robin Hood, and, even when it was worn as intended, I could be Inspector Fabian of Scotland Yard

At other times, when wearing the kitchen colander on my head I was a Roman soldier, a knitted balaclava could become a flying helmet and then I became Biggles. The rest of me, like most small children at the time, was grey and colourless. Shirt, pullover, flannel shorts and long socks, all in grey, so they didn't show the dirt. Those were grey times, when children didn't change their clothes as often as now. But with the right headgear, my imagination took care of the rest.

I last remembered wearing the hat when I was seven, at a concert that we neighbourhood children had organised for the RSPCA and in a part of our garden, known to us as "The Land". As the only boy, I had been picked as the compere, and the five girls were going to do a selection of poetry and stuff that they had learned at their dance classes. Even a skipping exhibition. I think we were proud of the fact that we had organised the event ourselves, though I suspect that Anne, Margot Belton's disdainfully older sister, probably gave us some begrudged advice.

I had decided to style myself on a popular comedian at the time called Arthur English, his shtick was to play the spiv or wide boy, a common phenomenon in those years just after the war. To achieve this, I wore the velvet trilby and pencilled on a thin moustache with my mother's eyebrow pencil. Unable to learn a script, I had decided to read some jokes from *Folsham's Book of Humour and Limericks*.

The audience, most of whom were parents or otherwise related to us, sat on a selection of garden chairs and some others co-opted from the dining room. It was a wonderful summer's day and the music, provided by Mr Belton's wind-up gramophone, carried, unamplified, on the warm still air. I had the responsibility of keeping it wound up and stopping Topper the spaniel from attacking it.

The only refreshment we offered was a lemonade, of sorts, that we had made with a luminous green sherbet powder. We thought it was delicious. My parents were away at the time, but my grandmother, in whose house we lived was in the audience and apologising to everyone for not providing tea. "They organised themselves, they insisted," she offered as an excuse.

The announcements seemed to go well, though I kept forgetting the stage names that the girls were using and kept having to ask them. Rosemary Kay's father found this very funny and though I couldn't understand why, I was glad of the laughs.

Mr Kay was the only man in the audience, and it transpired that he had earlier attended a successful and well provisioned business lunch. Mr Kay was in a very expansive mood. This, of course, was totally out of my experience, I just thought that he found me funny and this encouraged me.

I had started with a song, I don't remember what it was. At that age I probably got the lyrics wrong, parroting what I thought I had heard on the Light Programme. This was acknowledged by polite applause. The limericks, however, did not seem to satisfy Mr Kay, who seemed to have confused me with someone called Max Miller. "Give us a rude one Max, give us something from the blue book," he called out. People started to snigger and raised eyebrows at each other.

Something rude, I thought, *I can do that*. All children can call upon slightly, let us say, disrespectful rhymes, that they share amongst themselves. So, I gave them:

"Mrs Brown went to town, with her knickers hanging down

Mrs Green saw the scene and put it in a magazine

Mrs Black had to pack, all her knickers in a sack."

Mr Kay said, "That's more like it, more like that, Maxie". The others had started to laugh, probably, I now realise, more at him than at me, but I was getting a taste for it and started inventing some of my own.

"Mrs Blue got the flu' .... 'cos the cat wee'd in her shoe

Mrs Yellow gave a bellow 'cos the cat pooh'd in her umbrella."

Then I started to remember things that my parents and their friends had found amusing, before someone noticed me listening and said *"pas devant les enfants"*. I had not understood these jokes, but these grownups might.

Mr Kay fell off his chair laughing and had to be helped back into it, this made everyone else laugh, and for the first time I experienced the high of having an audience with you, I was flying. What I had not heard or realised was that the merriment was drowning out my grandmother's urgent whispers "Anthony... Anthony. That's enough... Anthony!"

Embarrassingly, it went on, but happily I cannot remember the details. Suffice to say, that my repertoire eventually ran out and the audience calmed down enough to watch Myfanwy Clarke do a sword dance with two bread knives.

To her credit my grandmother never mentioned or criticised me for my performance and the RSPCA gained 10 shillings and 6 pence.

Realisation came thirty-five years later at a reunion with Mrs Belton, our next-door neighbour in those days. "Anthony was an excitable child," she explained to my first wife. "The children had a concert in his garden, it was hilarious. Phillip Kay was drunk, and Anthony came out with all these rude jokes, his grandma tried to stop him, but Anthony wouldn't listen." We all laughed but I think she was very embarrassed. At that moment, thirty-five years too late, so was I.

Is That Really Me?

Nick Nicholson

I really hate the sound of my own voice, and those of you who know me as a man who never hesitates to venture an opinion or to refuse the opportunity to speak into a microphone, will be surprised to hear that.

This only becomes a problem when my utterances are recorded and played back to me. If I were reading this to you, I would imagine myself to be delivering it in standard RP. However, if it were played back to me, I would hear traces of all the places that I have lived in over the last seventy-five years. Also, despite my ability to sing baritone, my speaking voice is a higher pitch than I would like.

There are distinct traces of Oxford, where I spent my adolescence. Not the superior and assured speech of an academic, but the combination of Midlands and Home Counties used by Oxonians. I no longer address people as *"moi ducks"*, certainly more *town* than *gown*.

Thirty years in a West Country regiment has inflicted on me a slight *Archers* type of Mummerset burr. Yet another consequence of my military service is having a loud voice. Often, as a civilian, I have been asked by people "Why are you shouting?" My genuine response that "I didn't realise that I was", is seldom believed and has led to unintended impressions of bullying.

My twelve years living in London has resulted in a tinge of the Estuary and a tendency towards Cockney idioms. This became something of a parody when I donned a policeman's helmet, saying things like, "don't give me any of your porkies". I was not alone in this; *The Sweeney* has a lot to answer for.

In the forties and fifties there was a distinguished Shakespearean actor (Felix Aylmer) who had a dignified and learned style of delivery. This led to him often being typecast as a judge in many film and television productions. Indeed, it became something of a joke in the Royal Courts of Justice and the Old Bailey that so many High Court judges were modelling themselves on him. It is not known if he was in on the joke or aware of his role as a template.

I would not mind having an accent, if my diction were good. But I would like it to be consistent and identifiable. Having been born in and spent the first eleven years of my life in Hull, I would like it to be a dependable and no-nonsense Yorkshire – the accent that my parents worked hard to eradicate in themselves. Sadly, this only re-appears in me on my rare visits up north. After the first twenty-four hours in the East Riding, I revert to using a short "a" and say "*grass*" like "*pass*", rather than "*arse*" and referring to ten-foots and ginnels.

I will admit to being something of a sociolinguistic chameleon, after a few weeks I can find myself adopting the cadence and interjections of the locals. I once had the unpleasant job of imparting some tragic news to my Northern Irish ex in-laws in several phone calls. In response to their expressions of sympathy I found myself making interjections such as "*aye*", "*aye rightly*" and "*a-ha*". My then and current wife, who thought them all very insincere, told me years later that listening to it infuriated her. Another "*sure*" and she would have screamed.

I keep reminding myself that what you say is more important than how you say it. I am a good mimic, so I could address some of these concerns, but would that really be me? Or would it be a telephone voiced version of me? Better stick to writing. For, unless it is dialogue, writing has no accent, or does it?

When Jack went over the top

Gillian Langton

Jack was a gangly Lancashire lad,
With a heartbreak smile and grey-green eyes,
His friends were all signing up in droves,
They'd heard the story, learnt the lies.
"Come with us Jack, we'll soon be back,
In time for Christmas is what they say.
It's for King and country, Jack, my lad,
You can't just sit at home and pray."

Jack thought of her, his chosen one,
The one he hoped to make his wife.
They'd made a promise sealed with a kiss,
How could he gamble with his life?
And when he told her, how she clung,
Her dark eyes pleading. Was he in jest?
Her smile never wavered but she felt
Her heart was shuddering in her breast.

So off they went, those lively lads,
Leaving their cobbled streets behind,
And all their friends and families came,
And brass band played as they watched them wind
Their glorious, rollocking, uniformed way,
And onto the train, and kiss goodbye,
With hoots and shouts and "here we go"
And "see you soon" and "Mother, don't cry!"

A last puff of steam, the train pulls out,
The handkerchiefs fluttering in the breeze
A face at the window and then they're gone.
"They're gone" said Ma, "He's gone, our Jack."
She knows in her heart he will never come back.
And oh his lover is pale and sad,
She works in the factory making shells,
But at night she lies down and dreams of Jack,
And hears the sweet peal of wedding bells.

The ponies that lived in the field near Jack
Are gone to the war. Will they ever come back?
Ma thinks how he loved them and gave them treats,
Apples and carrots and sometimes sweets,
He loved them nuzzling in his hand.
 But now they pull guns instead of the plough,

And struggle through mud in a foreign land.

One day, Ma is stirring a pot on the stove,
Through her half closed eyes she is stirring a stew.
"When's our Jack coming home Ma?" the little lad asks,
Her eyes jolt open as she comes to,
"I don't know my darling, he'll need a good rest,"
Her heart is juddering in her breast,
"And wash your hands, just look at you!"
Some time later the telegram comes, and the telegraph boy
hands it over to Ma.
She reads, says nothing, goes back to the range,
After all, what else could she possibly do?

And the lad on his bike thinks it rather strange,
It was just as if she already knew.

And what of our Jack who won't ever come back,
The one with the laughing grey-green eyes?
And how did he feel when the order came through?
Did he still believe in the same old lies?
Did he think of his home, of his love, of his Ma?
Of the babes unborn, including his own,
The sad girls waiting, the mothers who cried,
The futures all stolen from those who died.

They were our future too, but Jack knew what to do,
And he said a small prayer for those who were there,
"Please God, let us live to the end of this day,
and God, make the killing stop now, this I pray"
But the past and the future are all entwined
And the killing goes on, will it never stop?
And we all lost out on that long ago day,
When Jack hauled himself over the top.

My Friend the Moon

Gillian Langton

Your light upon the window-sill beside my bed
Lit many childhood nights, awake, alone at last, and parent-free.
I sat for hours bathing in the gentle glow,
Reading, scribbling, dreaming of what I did not know.

Yesterday, out walking, I stopped, looked up beyond the trees,
and saw you hiding in plain sight,
So pale and thin, transparent even, hardly there,
Your former self a ghost of silver-white.
Sneaking a peek at our daytime goings -on,
Our to-ing and fro-ing, our scurrying, our noise,
Our busy self-importance and our helplessness.

But then, last night in darkness, your brilliant light
Forced me to raise my eyes. You were right
Overhead, and there, my arms full of damp washing,
I stood beneath you,
Humbled by your glorious light,
The full moon shining as I remembered you.
You seemed to be saying, Look! see what I truly am !
Do you remember me from childhood days?
We saw each other then with such a steady gaze.
And I am still here, tugging at your tides, your ebb and flow,
Pulling at your waters and your blood.
And I answered Yes, you are still there I know,
Still sailing through the Heavens with your ancient grace,

Oh lovely Moon with your familiar face.

Stay shining through my life, my friend the Moon.

Moonlight Encounter

Gillian Langton

It was a soft moonlit June night. The two lovers stood opposite each other on the lawn, the moonlight seemingly glowing over the trees and dusting them with silver. Slowly they began to move, making a circular, stately dance upon the grass, eyes only for each other.

There was something magical in their movements, each mirroring the other. Closer and closer they moved like partners in some ancient ritual of love and longing.

The girl watching upstairs from the bedroom window held her breath, completely mesmerized by the moonlit scene. The lovers were still circling ever closer when a large cloud drifted across the sky, veiling the moon and causing dark shadows to fall across the lawn. The watching girl had the uncomfortable feeling she was intruding on a private meeting, and this, coupled with her increasing sleepiness, caused her to let the curtain fall across the window and snuggle down in her bed.

Outside, the veil lifted from the moon and the garden was flooded again with silver light. The two hedgehogs were still circling and nearly closed in a cautious embrace. Many years later the girl, now an old woman, would recall the scene on that moonlit night long ago when two small creatures enacted the oldest story of grace and passion in a suburban garden.

The Song of the Microbead

Gillian Langton

I am a plastic microbead, I'm really very small,
Most people never heard of me, or know I'm there at all.
I hide inside your body scrub, your soap and cream and gel,
I'm sometimes in your toothpaste so I'm in your mouth as well.
I work my way through pipes and drains and rivers running
free,
I just keep going till at last I reach the open sea,
And there, while swimming through the deep I'm swallowed
by the whales,
The porpoises and dolphins, and the fish with shiny scales,
I get inside them all, my dears, with thousands of my mates,
And when the fish are caught my dears, I may land on your
plates.
You'll eat me unawares, my dears, I just go round and round,
I'll still be here for years to come when you are in the ground.
And so I'll say my farewell my dears, for it is sad but true,
I just go on for evermore,
Can't say the same for you.

Togetherness

Pat Fletcher

That morning she awoke feeling as though all her prayers had been answered, without having had to utter a word, wish or hope.

A dream. Her mother had appeared before her – her beautiful, gorgeous mother – filled to overflowing with infectious love.

It had been difficult. Both had reverted to small talk. It was the best they could do. Small talk held together with harnessed tears of unspoken words: together – and apart. Mother, daughter, daughter, mother, entwined for all time. Through pain, hurt, grief, laughter, pride, joy and sheer mischievousness, some shared, much not. Separation and being separate had become the norm. No matter what, whenever they were brought together once more, a new togetherness arose, dancing awhile amongst the scraps of dialogue – ashes of discomfort. It was a togetherness like no other. A spark that would bring them both back home to stay awhile in each other's lives.

This time was different.

I had managed to get to see her before lockdown. Silly really, because the virus was out there, everywhere. And there I was travelling to see her by train. All was well. What would usually have been a busy commute was eerily empty. Devoid of life. I say I got to see her, but it was through a downstairs window. Yes, the home had closed their doors just the day before. It was awful. The worst visit ever for us both. Ridiculously close and yet… It broke our hearts to part, yet the smiles and love remained intact. Would we see each other again? Would this be our last time together?

The stillness brought us together more vividly enthralled with love than was realisable, yet there it was, where it had always been. A dream of deepest love like no other, beyond time itself. Immortal love. Delicate, unwavering, in a life of constant flux, two souls being held together in a lifelong embrace… beyond – and not …x

Vera Elizabeth White, née Broughton 11.3.1928 – 5.3.2021

Amazing lady, woman, spirit, heart and soul

My mum

Empty?

Pat Fletcher

The meeting is over
all going, their presence melting
away along the corridors and down the stairs.
Some doors opening, a lull, then swinging closed.
A full stop in time.
A separation.

The clock tells the time,
but only when I choose.
Two short minutes ago
one made a move, then the other.
A bit of a shuffle here,
a moving of things,
a closing of their notes,
glances from one to another.
The shift in sound, a Geronimo! Of sorts.

Lives in transition away and toward,
away from here and towards there.
Already elsewhere?
Trailing off out of mine, making headway into another.
Everything done, dusted, sorted.
What was it that kept us together?

And so we part,
space revealing itself between
spreads inside.
Space, relaxing,
space to be,
to breathe and to be.
Devoid of all busy-ness,
yet full.
Full of me…

Today, the 18th of October

Pat Fletcher

Apparently, the 18th of October is the most likely last fine day of the year. As it turns out, 2020's is splendid!

Here are some words by yours truly in homage to the sun
Today, the 18th of October
One day in history
One day in life
The sun has seen them all.
What might she think as she raises her head
casting dawn upon the morn
What's happened here?
What's appeared, what's gone?
The happenings are so many.

Today marks the day
she shines at her best
for maybe some time to come.
It's time to ready
all her autumnal energy
to flood the earth in this
her finest finale.

For before too long
she'll spend less time here
in the lives she's come to know.
Reacquainting herself
with those emerging from darkness,
thawing softly, nourished in her glow.

(Thank you Jackie Juno and the Totnes Library Writers Group
for inspiring these words)

Living

Pat Fletcher

Sometimes, just sometimes
I haven't the first clue
about how to go about
living my life

Then sometimes, other times
things happen.
Beautiful things happen
that blow me away

It's no small wonder that
sometimes, just sometimes
I haven't the first clue.

What if

Pat Fletcher

What if we were to be free of all fetters?
Would we run amok, raping, pillaging, wreaking havoc wher-
ever we tread?
Or would we instead…
Become at one with nature, in nature, naturally flowing with all
living…
… in which there is the predator, constantly steady
… to pounce on anything too innocent or ready…

What if humanness were gentle, warm, nurturing?
Still alive with life's sparkle, life's fire
entwined in love, passion warmed, softened with love's glow.
Serious compassion living and breathing, living being.
Passions, flare, fire aglow with love in the flow
In all we are, in all we do, wherever we go.

What if? and Why not!

They say it can't be so

… What if there were no smallness inside
In which to hide?

(Thank you to Harula Ladd for the inspiration – from your
'What If', to mine)

Winting

Pat Fletcher

The heating's off
Oh now it's on again.
Wardrobe's looking bleak,
still our layers pile on many and thick
when will this season end?

Rains intense, unrelenting
blotting all hope of springlike plenty
Long gone the dreams of
summer's gaze,
glistening through springtime's haze.
And nature, lost, what a frenzy!

Blackbirds scrabbling through treasure troves
when respite comes a-calling.
Spring in the air… and not.
On again, off again,
still the winds blow too strong.
Icy bites beneath the bluster,
chilling, thrilling, drilling to the core.
Just what exactly is the score!

There really is nowhere to go
we fluster, bluster, but this is it.
The sap starts its rising
pricking life to parts in peaceful slumber,
"Let it go, let all rip, go on do it anyway!"
After all there is life to live –
no matter the weather.

Urban Decay

Pat Fletcher

It's spring,
nature breaks through.
Fresh, new innocence unaware of what lies ahead.
The onslaught is too much,
too overpowering.

Glimpses remain and can be found,
for the safe and the sound of mind,
but even the birds' souls shrink
away, unable to play
In the dark, dull darkness.

Harvest Moon

Fiona Barker

Shhhh…
Stillness steals across pasture, straw and stone.
As September days shorten,
The sunset rising of our sister satellite
Allows precious extra hours
Of industry.
But now a softer light settles,
Sliding shadows amongst the stalks.
Ghost grasses
Whisper secrets of harvests past.
A mouse scurries,
A sudden susurration,
Escaping owlish intentions.
Summer,
Subdued by celestial caress,
Slips towards sleep.

The Lowe Library

Fiona Barker

We came in awe to the Lowe Library,
On the cusp of stories as yet untold.
We were products of comprehensive modernity,
Abruptly displaced from our brave new world
Into an ancient one that demanded respect.
From our schools of sharp, red brick
We came to cloisters of soft, honeyed stone.
Here were panelled walls,
Heavy with a hundred years of history and beeswax.
Our tubular desks with plywood tops
Were replaced with dependable oak,
Inscribed signatures on their underside,
Instead of chewing gum.
No faceless plastic chairs,
So easy to stack,
No textured surface to discourage the fidgeting of bored bums.
Here was red leather,
Worn soft and smooth by generations of learned behinds.
Climbing the spiral spine of this august institution,
There was no scent of now
But the intoxicating smell of hot dust and collected wisdom.
There were no shouts echoing down concrete covered-ways
But cathedral bells drifting through open casements
And murmured voices floating up from the courtyard below,
Whispered questions and confidences.
In that library, we came to know ourselves and the world.

We came in awe but it did not last.
Irreverent imps from who knows where,
We knew it by another name
Because of extra lessons learned there.
We were so lucky.
If only we had known it then.

Note: The Lowe Library is part of the University College, Durham.

These are the Gifts of the Sea

Fiona Barker

These are the gifts of the sea, my girl.
They carry stories from far-off lands
To this secret shore
And tell a different tale to every traveller.
They have been smoothed into silence
But need only a touch to sing their song.
Here is one as soft as silk,
A dragon's egg,
Awaiting a hopeful hatcher.
Here is a scale from a mermaid's tail,
Shed in the flurry of escape
From a distant foe.
This one has a hole,
Through which the future
Is foretold
And perhaps it is possible to view,
Out across the sea,
A pirate's destiny.
Here is a mini moon,
A fallen fragment of the universe,
Made for magic.
And here is another
That has trapped all the greens and blues
Of the sea and sky.
And last, here is ours,
One larger with a smaller held within,

Mother and child,
Composite.
Set in stone.

Plutonic Relationship

Fiona Barker

To be or not to be, the bard has said.
Do all the planets ask that of themselves?
For Pluto, certainly, it must be apt
You scruffy, misshapen ball of rock,
Out whirling round me at such pace.
I wonder if you ever stop to think
About the very purpose of your flight.
When first discovered, what a marvel then
Within the planetary pantheon
To be so welcomed; planet number nine!
How disappointing to be later cut
And demoted from the celestial ranks
To minor planet of the Kuiper belt.
You're not to be but I still think of you.

Orrery

Fiona Barker

Observing planetary orbits,
Recognised reductions of real revolutions,
Regulated distillations of complexity.
Exactitude,
Respecting my command.
Years mapped in moments.

The Butterfly Cage

Marie Chesham

Vanessa went into the kitchen and put the kettle on. She was staring out of the window when she saw it. The fox was in the garden again. It was moving slowly through the overgrown shrubs, its dew dampened fur just visible through the fresh spring growth. As she watched, with a rip of speed, it leapt out. Its front paws stretched out towards a Red Admiral butterfly. The butterfly, with a nonchalant flap of its wings, evaded the grasping paws with ease. The fox, disappointed, sat down, returning Vanessa's stare. It was a large animal, its fur a dark brownish red, the long full brush curling round its front paws. She had tried to make friends with it, but the fox had remained indifferent even to the food she had offered. She switched off the kettle and poured the water onto her tea bag and when she looked up again the fox had gone.

Later, she decided to go up into the attic to retrieve some files for her current history research project. As she opened the box, she noticed something nearby. It looked like a small bird cage, the white painted metal dirty and rusted. She hadn't noticed it before, perhaps Tom, her husband had found it and put it down near the box when he was last in the attic. She picked it up and holding it by the hook at the top, twirled it round, years of dust fanning out into the hot air of the attic. Looking closer she saw the corpse of a butterfly resting inside on the bottom, just visible in a bed of grey dust. It had obviously been there a long time as the colours were so faded it was hard to tell what species it was. Tom would probably know, even in its degraded state, as butterflies were his passion. She must remember to ask him when he came home. Her eye was then caught by something in the far corner, a very faint glimmer of metal but again covered in drifts of dust and old spiders' webs. She put the cage down and went over to see what it was. It looked like some sort of slim wooden cabinet with several drawers. She blew some of the dust away and saw antique brass handles. She carefully opened the top drawer and inside, in a glass case, she saw through a thin film of dust row upon row of dead butterflies, pinned in perfect alignment. They were all Red Admirals. She wasn't too keen on spiders' webs, but this made her shudder even more. Blowing the rest of the dust away she could see them, the vibrant colour patterns preserved through what must be years since their unnatural deaths. She noticed that there was one space at the end of the top row. There was a pin hole and a faint shadow, the shape of a butterfly with its wings outstretched. She suddenly felt quite distressed, cold, and rushed back to the ladder. Just as she went to put her foot on the first rung, she thought she saw a shadow; a long dark shape across the wall; she stopped for a moment and turned towards it. There was nothing. She must have imagined it; the cabinet and its contents had obviously unsettled her. It was then that she realised she had meant to bring the bird cage or whatever it was. It could wait for another time, but she would make sure Tom got rid of that cabinet of murdered butterflies. She quickly descended the ladder and shut the attic hatch door.

They had bought the house two years ago, charmed by its odd hotch potch of varying architectural periods and fashions and the large Victorian conservatory facing the long, descending garden which had made an imposing addition. It was in here, once it had been cleaned and restored, that Vanessa hung what Tom had told her was a butterfly cage. Tom had been in no doubt that the long dead butterfly was another Red Admiral. After searching around the attic, he had also found an old butterfly net, a little motheaten, not far from the cabinet.

Vanessa had not succeeded in getting Tom to throw out the butterfly cabinet and eventually they had reached a compromise; Tom put it in his study, the old drawing room, and Vanessa told him he would have to clean the room himself as she could not bear to think about the butterflies. He thought it was an interesting collection as all the specimens showed a very subtle variation on the standard colour patterns of the species. What was strange was that the top drawer had been open when he had gone to get the cabinet from the attic. Vanessa knew she had closed it.

Vanessa wondered if the butterflies had been collected in the beautiful water meadow that bordered the end of their garden. She had seen the layered purple haze of orchids and ragged robin in the late spring followed by many more wildflowers throughout the summer. The water meadow was as full of butterflies as it was of flowers. The Red Admiral, that the fox had so desperately wanted to catch, had been the only butterfly she had ever seen in their nectar rich garden.

She was working in the conservatory one morning when she saw the shadow again. It seemed to flit around the room, just near or past the potted flowers. But what was casting the shadow? There was only her in the house. Again, she felt cold only this time it was as if the sensation was slowly enfolding her, she tried to move but it was as if a paralysis had come over her. And then she saw it, the fox. It was right by the conservatory doors, standing almost upright with its two front paws up against the glass. It wasn't looking at her. She followed the stare of its bright amber eyes and saw the shadow which was now totally still on the ceiling just above the butterfly cage. When she was able to move, she saw the fox had gone, melted away into the shrubbery but despite it having rained that night, there was no sign of any paw prints on the window or even the lawn. She looked at the butterfly cage and she saw that the shadow had also gone but at the bottom was a dead Red Admiral. It appeared to be quite fresh, but how had it got into the cage? What had cast the shadow and where had the dead butterfly come from?

Next day, after a troubled night's sleep full of shadows and fleeting glimpses of black, red and white patterned wings that flitted in and out of her dream, she got up early. Instead of going into the kitchen to make a mug of tea as she normally did, she went straight into the conservatory. The delicate body of the butterfly was still in the cage. She gently lifted it out and went into Tom's study. Carefully placing it on his desk she went over to the cabinet. She was surprised to see that the top drawer was half open. Tom would never have done that as the exposure to the light would ruin the specimens. She lifted the butterfly case out and laid it on his desk beside the frail lifeless body. As she released the metal catches, she saw a pin lying at the bottom of the case. She did not know how she was going to do it, but she knew she had to; her hand shaking, she carefully placed the butterfly at the end of the top row. She took a deep breath and pieced its slender body with the pin. It was a perfect fit over the pale grey shadow mark. And then she saw a shadow drift up from underneath the butterfly's body and watched as it seemed to float away and out through the open window.

That night she dreamt she saw a small boy with a butterfly net chasing a Red Admiral through the water meadow, his slight frame casting a dark long shadow in the bright sun light. A large fox with brownish red fur was running by his side. The boy, laughing, stopped for a moment and looked towards her. He waved and shouted out "goodbye" and then he and the fox ran through the long slender grass, the boy's hand still waving until they both disappeared at the water's edge.

A Dangerous Temptation

Marie Chesham

The mouse looked out from the hole under the large, gnarled tree root. There was a slight breeze coming towards him and he twitched his whiskers, sampling the layers of spring aromas. He wasn't sure. He darted back through the hole and into the chamber he had dug out for himself with its snug bed of golden, dry hay, the stalks carefully worked to provide a tiny access hole. He rushed around, rearranged his neat pile of seeds and then sat inhaling the warm perfume of the hay, the earthy scent of the rich dark compacted soil, the sharp scent of the brittle seeds.

He made his way back up the dark passageway; paused where the hole opened out under the tree. He looked each way and then back again, he raised his brown head and he looked straight out, his enormous eyes shining brightly in the fading light. He sniffed and sniffed; if he was quick, he was sure he would be all right. The cache of food he had stumbled on in the wildwood was tempting him back for another visit. He knew it belonged to the grey squirrel, but he reckoned on being faster than the squirrel if it came back unexpectedly.

He darted out onto the woodland floor, following his own laid paths with an unfailing discipline. He was nearly there, back to the spot where he had lifted out the beautiful, dark brown hazelnut from its shallow burial in the leaf mould. This was it, this was the place. The smell of the copper brown nuts was overwhelming as he roved backwards and forwards, but which would be the easiest to take? He stopped. He sniffed and his whiskers resonated with delight. He scraped and pushed and there it was, just a little more effort, another scrape, another push and he would have it. In that moment he lost himself in the sheer anticipation of a bite of the creamy, white nut and the unseen tawny owl, swooped down in a silent fan of feathers. The mouse was elevated up, up through the canopy of the wildwood. The prize, the beautiful hazelnut, lay uncovered, ready for the taking but with each wing beat, it became smaller and smaller.

The owl, startled by a loud noise on its homeward journey to its hungry chicks, lost its grip of the tiny mouse, who fell forever, down through the trees, landing with a bump onto a soft bed of autumn leaf litter. He should have taken more care to watch for danger. He knew that now. Another day, another lesson learned.

I'm All of a Twitch

Thelma Portch

Bird watchers are known as twitchers,
It's an up-market thing to be.
Now, I'll be a curtain twitcher
There's nothing else open to me.

When you've gone past your middle nineties
You'll have given up 'going all out'
Cos you just cannot scramble
Through bog and through bramble
With your field glasses bumping about.

I can still tell a rook from a raven
But I've set all that knowledge aside
And my living-room is my haven
~ I'm going to rename it my hide.

I'll be lurking behind my lace curtain
In the heart of our village square
And I'll see what goes on there, for certain
Cos my eyes will be everywhere!

The Conservative Club is right at the hub
My glasses are trained on its door,
The Post Office too, is well within view
And our local Co-op store.

So I'll always be knowing
Who's coming and going
And, maybe, a good deal more.

I shall study their feeding habits
Cos I'll see what they take home for tea,
If they're having a fling
Whilst they're out on a wing
It will not come as news to me!

Then I'll write up my notes in the evening
When they're all coming home to roost
I'll be drinking a gin whilst I'm logging them in.
It will give me a bit of a boost.

But it's all just a flight of my fancy
I've been talking a whole lot of hype
And I haven't a clue
To what neighbours may do
~ I'm not the inquisitive type.

Sew --- What??

Thelma Portch

The sight of a bobbin can set me throbbin'
It makes me feel terribly low,
With needles and cotton my efforts were rotten
And everyone told me so.
I was always a slattern when reading a pattern
So I cut that out long ago.
I was no good at knitting
And so it seemed fitting to cast off whatever I made,
Though I gave it a whirl, did some plain and some purl
I never quite made the grade.
Now I get all my tops from the high street shops
Where I buy all my clothes ready-made.

La Donna Immobilized

Aria for OAP on public transport
Thelma Portch

Give up your seat to me
Because I'm elderly.
Front seats are meant to be
For the elderly.
Look at me, you'll agree
I am elderly!
Now, have I made it clear?
Get your arse out of here!
Move further down the bus
You are not one of us.
Front seats are meant to be
For the elderly.

Caught in a Shower

Thelma Portch

She was whiling away an hour in her walk-in bath and shower
And only half awake
When a swish and a slide and a downward glide
Found her caught in the coils of a snake.

Though she hardly knew what she ought to do in this dangerous
situation
As she sat in the toils of those silvery coils
She was hoping to meet with temptation.

I hardly need mention
That such an attention was drastically overdue
For at this stage she had reached an age when serpents
Don't bother with you.

Her matronly figure had lost its vigour
Her skin was all wrinkly and lined
But it wasn't too late to meet with a mate
Who would value her for her mind.

Though she didn't feel bold cos the water was cold
And she knew she was over-exposed.
In spite of the chill it gave her a thrill
Well, she wondered what might be proposed.

But the moment soon passed – how could it last?
And yet she likes to recall
That fleeting chance of a new romance
When the shower cable fell off the wall!!

93 in the Shade at Costa del North Street

Thelma Portch

They've set up a hot-tub just over the wall.
Whilst my neighbours were frolicking there
I was sitting here, feeling so out of it all
Though I hadn't a thing I could wear.

Well I'd managed to find my bikini suit
And also my one-piece with skirt,
But neither would fit, cos I've put on a bit
So I'd have to dive in in my shirt.

Every table and chair has a festive air
They've got flags on their whirly-bird line,
The state of my garden can hardly compare
~ I've only got knickers on mine.

When I opened my back door and called out "Olay"!
As I brandished a bottle of wine
They said 'You're just nosey – we don't want your Rosé
We've plenty to drink, we'll be fine!'

Then I muttered "Caramba" and started to samba
I was humming a catchy refrain
And my hip joints were clicking like castanets flicking
As I whirled round again and again!

Till they yelled "Cool it Grandma, give up on that Samba
You're driving us all insane!
Be off you old shocker, get back on your rocker
And stick to your purl and your plain."

So I'm sitting here soaking my feet in a bowl
And drinking a nice cup of tea
Well out of the clamour, away from the glamour
It's a sensible option for me!

Contributors

David Barker

David Barker is the author of three Climate Fiction thrillers – the Gold trilogy (Bloodhound Books) – and gives talks on water shortages and climate change. Prior to writing full time, David worked in the City as an economist where his fascination with commodity shortages began.

He attended the Faber Academy in 2014 and, more recently, completed a scriptwriting course with the National Writing Centre. When not writing thrillers or scripts, David likes to create stories for younger readers and joined the Society of Children's Book Writers and Illustrators in 2018.

You can find out more about David and his writing at: https://davidbarkerauthor.co.uk

Fiona Barker

Married, middle-aged mum of one. Reluctant to rhyme but longing for alliterative loveliness. Positively potty about picture books! Author of *Danny and the Dream Dog* and *Setsuko and the Song of the Sea* (both out now with Tiny Tree Children's Books).

Ruth Brooks

Ruth is a published author having written two books: *A Slow Passion* and *Nine Lives*. She has always enjoyed writing – anything from a shopping list to a book. She loves reading, natural history, gardening, science, and shared meals with friends.

Marie Chesham

Marie has worked in both the public and service industry sectors including roles in sales, marketing, and public relations. Retirement has given her more time to work in the garden and to explore writing fiction – in particular short stories. Her love of flora and fauna is often reflected in her work. The sights and sounds encountered walking in the beautiful and diverse Devon landscape provide a constant source of inspiration.

Barbara Childs

After a career as an art teacher and printmaker, Barbara started writing about fifteen years ago. She joined the Totnes Library Writers Group in 2014 and contributed poems to the first *Gallimaufry* anthology the following year.

Carole Ellis

Carole has been a book-keeper, a baker and a teacher. An Essex girl by birth, she is now Totnesian by choice. Her precious spare time is spent walking the Devon countryside or swimming off its coast. Carole has been a member of the Library Writers Group since its inception, and writes when the spirit moves! She has also been a co-presenter of Life with a Literary Slant for local radio station, Soundart.

Pat Fletcher

"Just go and write a book!" blurted an exasperated lecturer.

Pat had left a 30-year career in corporate finance management to study for a degree. Having a strong community spirit with a knack for spotting injustice and a passion for nature, she felt it was an itch that needed scratching. Whilst the course was good, the library inspired.

The written word – both a gift and responsibility.

A busy body, at home in Devon, Pat enjoys practising her Reiki and Transformational therapy, writing her blog and self-help book. Relaxation is meeting friends over coffee, gardening, walking, sailing and unearthing hidden gems.

Fiona Green

Fiona was the 4th generation of her family born in India.

Following schooling across the world, she eventually settled in London where she married a poet/publisher, had children and taught.

She became the Divisional Coordinator of Support Services in Southwark 1987 – 1990.

On leaving that service, she trained to be a Gestalt couples' psychotherapist, which she practised from 1990 – 2012, when she retired to her hometown of Totnes to paint and write.

Anna Hattersley

Anna grew up in the Netherlands, but now lives on the edge of Dartmoor. She misses cycling on the flat and *poffertjes* (tiny, puffy pancakes), but loves running on the moor and swimming in its rivers. She joined the Totnes Library Writers Group to encourage herself to write more and found a lovely group of people to enjoy writing alongside.

Jackie Juno

Jackie is a writer, poet and performer living on the edge of Dartmoor.

A multiple poetry slam winner, including Glastonbury Festival

Slam 2017, and reaching the National Poetry Slam finals at the Albert Hall in 2018, she held the title Bard of Exeter 2011-2012 and Grand Bard of Exeter 2012-2019.

She teaches creative writing online and in person, and loves inspiring new writers.

Jackie is also lead singer and lyricist with psychedelic rock band The Invisible Opera Company of Tibet. She has a bit of a map fetish, and is so painfully hip that she needs a new one.

Harula Ladd

Harula is a popular poet on the Devon scene, the current Exeter Slam Champion and one quarter of Spork Up! – as well as helping Clive's make pies in her non-writing time! Original, transformative, and possessing of a unique emotional intelligence, it's been said that Harula's poetry wraps itself around you with the warmth of one of her mum's brilliant handmade cardigans.

Gillian Langton

A graduate of the Royal College of Music, Gillian Langton worked at a psychiatric hospital as assistant music therapist and studied music therapy at a Steiner course in Berlin. She has worked as a piano teacher for ILEA and privately, and was accompanist for the Isle of Wight Cantata Choir. She helped to start and organise a music festival in Ventnor, her home town for many years. She also ran a choir in a day centre for psychiatric patients living in the community.

She now lives in Totnes where she continues her interests and involvement in music and in the writing group.

Caroline Lodge

Caroline writes in many genres: short stories, poetry, her bookish blog (www.bookword.co.uk), articles for local magazines, academic papers, co-authoring several non-fiction books and has a novel nestling in a drawer. She is currently exploring publishing. She is a founder member of the Totnes Library Writers Group, enjoying the support it provides and the opportunities for learning such as performance, anthologies, the festival of writing and the programme of workshops.

Anne Morris

Anne Morris started writing as a child, one wet seaside holiday, and has done so off and on ever since. She changed direction from a career working with people; moved to France and took up freelance journalism. Since her return she's been writing varied fiction and compiles and edits a newsletter for a local conservation group.

Under the Spindle Tree was inspired by a friend who loves to travel. It's part of a project started in lockdown with fellow writer Wendy Watkins, sharing their work inspired by paintings.

Julie Mullen

Julie Mullen trained at The Webber Douglas Academy of Dramatic Art and worked as an actor from 1989-2009 working on stage, television and radio. Credits include *The Bill, Trial & Retribution, Brookside, Coronation Street, Wing and A Prayer*. She was the voice of *Maltesers* for television. In 2009 she took up with poetry creating *Erotic Poetry For Vegans & Vegetarians*. Brian Patten wrote "Does for sprouts what Wordsworth did for daffodils." She took her one woman show to The Edinburgh Fringe receiving ****
(4 stars) and was poet in residence at The Pleasance Theatre in

Edinburgh for two years running. She loves the library group of Totnes and all the encouragement they give.

Anthony (Nick) Nicholson

Yorkshireman Anthony "Nick" Nicholson left his private school after a report "He is wasting our time and your money". Since then he has had a career that includes service in the Devonshire and Dorset Regiment, as Head Porter of an Oxford college and a girls' school.

Retiring in 2010, Nick became a volunteer with an animal charity and a member of the U3A. A keen amateur military and social historian, he is on the committee of ABBPAST and is involved with the Guildhall and St Mary's Church in Totnes. He is still trying to educate himself.

Nick writes short stories brimming with voices from his past.

Ann Pelletier-Topping

Originally from the French-speaking side of Montreal, Canada, Ann Pelletier-Topping now lives in Totnes. She's a keen late-starter poet whose poem *Granddaughter Moves In* won second prize in the National Poetry Competition (2019). Her poems have appeared in *Ambit* (2021) and in anthologies, such as *New Contexts 1* by Coverstory books (2021) and Moor Poets IV (2018). She's in the process of putting together a pamphlet. She loves dancing hip-hop and ballet even if she's not very good at it.

Thelma Portch

Very old Devonian, born in St Marychurch, Torquay in 1924, now lives in Ipplepen. Lifetime interests: literature and outdoor sports – can still enjoy the former, but may have to give up on sporting activities. Now enjoys writing and performing verses of Totally Tasteless Topics for All Occasions.

Paul Skinner

Paul worked as a chartered building surveyor. Now retired, he is taking the opportunity to write on more creative topics.

He has been able to visit Africa several times on small group safaris.

The word safari means journey in Swahili, but it is so much more. A true adventure often of an unpredictable nature and an opportunity to experience a very different way of life on a very different continent, get off the beaten track and see the real Africa. Paul's stories are of true events which he enjoys sharing with you.

Wendy Watkins

Wendy, having spent most of her life as a psychologist and psychotherapist in South Africa, was drawn to Britain by the Isle of Iona, and to Devon by a course at Schumacher College. She says if you want to know any more she'd be happy for you to imagine something like a Rorschach inkblot, and interpret it in a playful way.

Abby Williams

Abby recently moved to Totnes and is a new member of the Totnes Library Writers Group. She began writing poetry at primary school in Yorkshire, and has never stopped putting pen to paper. She writes poetry and short stories, and has novel-shaped ambitions. Taking a break after having spent 20 years as a creative copywriter, Abby is now halfway through an MA in Creative Writing.